THE RUNAWAY BREEDER

Alana Dyer

Copyright © 2020 Alana Dyer

All rights reserved

The characters and events portrayed in this book are fictitious. Any similarity to real persons, living or dead, is coincidental and not intended by the author.

No part of this book may be reproduced, or stored in a retrieval system, or transmitted in any form or by any means, electronic, mechanical, photocopying, recording, or otherwise, without express written permission of the publisher.

ISBN-13: 979-8-6732-4380-0

Cover design by: Alana Dyer
Printed in the United States of America

*This novel is deadicated to all the people who believed in me,
who kept motivating me to complete my first novel and who
kept saying that I will succeed even when I felt like I would fail.*

THE RUNAWAY BREEDER

By: Alana Dyer

CHAPTER 1

I sit in front of my mirror, my reflection staring back at me. My straight chestnut-coloured hair **is** piled on top of my head into a perfect bun, and the off-the-shoulder blush coloured top and high-waisted black lace skirt adorn my body, hopefully portraying me as a confident young she-wolf ready to take on her role in this pack.

Last month, I had just turned sixteen, the age a wolf finds their role in their pack and—possibly—their mate. It is the time when all wolves are deemed "adults" in our community, when a she-wolf can choose to give up school and start a family with her mate if she so desires. In the eyes of the werewolf nation, any wolf aged sixteen who has shifted to their wolf form is able to take on responsibility in furthering the success of their pack, with their Alphas designating their roles at the pack meeting on the first day of each month. Since I had missed out on last month's meeting due to my birthday being three days after the last pack meeting, I was unable to obtain my pack position. But today, I will be taking my place as a functioning adult in Pine Paw.

I couldn't help but smile at my reflection in excitement at the prospect of working and gaining respect from all; this thrill lifted my mood. My eyes shot over to the picture of my cousin, Chris, and I taped to the mirror. I take a deep breath and remind myself that my cousin will be there to support me no matter what role I received from the Alpha. Just after my birthday, when I first shifted into wolf form, Chris and I had gone for a run in the forest surrounding our territory. His idea was to get me accustomed to being on four legs instead of two. I remember Chris' black wolf form towering over my blue-white fur with black-tipped paws in the warm early-spring sunlight that the month of May had to offer that day, and the annoyance I felt knowing that I still have a few more years to continue growing into my wolf form while he could easily take me down. I look like a pup compared to my cousin, but being able to run around the territory and enjoy the early morning sun in wolf form felt incredible. There's no better feeling for a werewolf than your four paws pounding on the forest floor with the smell of the new leaves on the trees, the crisp pine, and the scattered scents of prey all around you. As a werewolf in wolf form, you feel complete in the forest. On that day, with Chris chasing me around like we were a pair of pups, I finally felt that sense of being whole.

"Laina, let's go before we're late," Chris yells impatiently, snapping me out of my thoughts. Chris's voice carries from the foyer where I know he waits, with a look of annoyance directed at me all the way up the stairs and down the hall to my room. Taking one last look at myself in the mirror and adjusting my shirt, I sigh, stand from my seat to look around for some shoes, and slip on a pair of knee-high black boots. I grab my cell phone from the desk beside the door while rushing out the room and scurry down the hallway. "I'm coming!" I reply back to my cousin, hurrying down the stairs to where he waits for me.

One thing that is annoying about Chris is his need to always be on time. Chris is what I like to call "time O.C.D." when it comes to being punctual. He would forget where he put his phone down and forget where his keys to his car were, but he will never fail to be early to a function or event. One example of Chris' habit of being early would be just a couple of years ago when we went to the movie theatre to see the live-action remake of "Beauty and the Beast." You can just imagine Jack and I waiting for an hour on Chris to find his wallet and car keys. He was running around the house like a chicken with its head chopped off only for the three of us to be miraculously two hours *early* to the movie because Chris had planned ahead that day for a late-night viewing. Needless to say, by the time the movie started to play, the bag of popcorn in my hands was a soggy, inedible mess for my pre-teen self to enjoy. I spent the entire movie with buttery hands and a bag of gross popcorn that I had since discarded on the floor.

"You look amazing," Chris gushes as I descend the final steps of the staircase and come to stand before him, doing a slight spin for my cousin to approve of my outfit. He has a look of pride in his amber eyes. I did everything with my cousin Chris, who acted as a brother, a parent, and a best friend. His approval meant the world to me, especially with today being the next step in my adult life as a functioning member of this pack. His mate, Jack, saunters over, giving me a once-over and a wink before snuggling into Chris's side with a contented smile on his face. "Thank you. You two look amazing as well," I reply with a blush as I take in the two complimenting each other with black slacks and button-down shirts of similar shades of blue.

Jack and Chris are the first openly gay mates in the pack that had come out about ten years ago. This pairing had started a bit of a rift amongst the pack when the two had found each other while on a run in the forest. I remember the excitement Chris had when he came home that night. He whisked my sleeping form out of my princess bed at ten o'clock at night to make me a plateful of chocolate chip pancakes just to talk about coming across a grey wolf during his run through the forest. He couldn't tell who this wolf was, only that he knew just by scent that the two of them were meant to be mates. At six years old, I remember sitting at the kitchen island, trying to stay awake with the knowledge of my cousin finding his prince charming and the scent of chocolate in the air. My parents were furious with my cousin, stating that a pup needed to sleep when they caught me red-handed with half a plate full of pancakes and a chattery Chris... But there was also a look of pride and excitement for him before they promptly ushered me into bed, while

Chris promised to tell me more tomorrow after a pack meeting. The next day at the pack meeting, Chris and Jack bumped into each other and, as if it were a scene out of a movie, Chris and Jack both exclaimed the word, "Mate!" Apparently, there was a huge uproar afterwards, with the pack in disbelief that two strong male wolves who could produce strong pups were mated to each other. For the next few days, I remembered the pack being tense and Chris explaining that he had to sneak out at night to see his mate because our pack was trying to keep Chris and Jack apart. I was heartbroken for my cousin, the man who told me stories about mates and how they are our other halves that we cannot live without. I remembered in kindergarten when this boy in class said his mother called Chris a freak and how I got in trouble for punching that kid in the face. It wasn't until the previous Alpha had stepped in and stopped any and all complaints before any other incidents occurred that could harm the pack. He admitted to everyone that same-sex mates are legal in the werewolf community and gave the chance for others to flourish in their love life. It was the Moon Goddess' blessing and intent to pair mates of the same-sex together, so who were they, the pack, to judge? With the Alpha giving Chris and Jack his blessing, more and more wolves who had admitted they had yet to find their mates soon came out as pairs. It soon became normal to see openly gay and lesbian couples around the pack, and I couldn't help but beam with pride at how accepting my pack is to change. Chris and Jack's relationship is quite sweet in a Romeo-and-Juliet kind of way in the beginning, with most of their families and pack members being against their mating. But the two persevered and kept strong. The only difference from Shakespeare's Romeo and Juliet is that no one died in our pack for my cousin to be happy with his mate.

"Now, let's hurry up before we are late. That is not a way to start off as a working member of this pack." Jack states a little too cheerily and grabs both Chris's and my wrist, dragging us out the door and into the car. The pack house is about a half an hour drive from where we live, used for meetings, special occasions and for warriors and wolves without mates to live with. If it weren't for Chris and Jack being my family and guardians, I would have been living at the pack house long ago since my parents' deaths. Slowly, the big mansion comes into view and the drive comes to an end, with the car coming to a stop in the parking lot and the three of us getting out in front of the old Victorian building. The nerves that have been missing this entire morning decide to make themselves present now while I climb out of the car, taking in the number of pack members hanging around.

"Remember, you are to mingle with the other wolves while the Alpha assigns you to your position. Who knows, maybe you are his soul mate," Chris encourages me, kissing my forehead before he and Jack walk away to join the other parents and guardians. I sigh sadly as I watch wolves my age talk to their parents one last time, wishing for once that my own had survived the rogue attack ten years ago so they could stand here and give me the advice to calm the nerves that send my heart into an unsteady rhythm. Shaking my head, I take a deep breath, sighing wistfully one last time before turning towards the building and heading inside with a brave smile on my face. Mom always told me to never show my true emotions when in a crowd of wolves. The strong prey on the weak, and I refuse to show any weakness.

As I enter the building, I am taken aback by the sheer amount of wolves my age, each ready to take on their responsibilities in this pack. Everyone is dressed in their best attire, hoping to leave a good impression as we all aim for the highest position possible. Many of the females have put a lot of consideration into their attire, switching their short shorts in the summer here for conservative dresses, blouses and slacks. Only the few females who aim to climb the pack hierarchy are dressed in revealing clothing. But we all have one position we do not want to obtain: the Breeder.

Breeders are the she-wolves assigned to become the pup

producers in the pack. Their job is to allow the mateless warriors of Pine Paw to breed them, with no say in who their partner is, during the current breeding period. Its intended purpose is to add more wolves to the pack population and bring about stronger wolves for the next generation. Many wolves believe it to be an honourable position a she-wolf can obtain, but we all know the truth. Once you become a Breeder, you are nothing more than a slave, a tool for men to use your body for their own pleasure while they rape you into producing the next lot of pups for the pack. If you ask me, it is a barbaric way to increase the pack's population, but the chosen she-wolves have no say in their position of a Breeder and no say in ending this barbaric job. To say that the slim chance of being chosen for this position scares me is an understatement. I am terrified for any she-wolf, myself included, that will receive this position, knowing that for the next chapter of their life, the she-wolf will be a slave until she produces the specified amount of twenty pups for the pack.

While everyone else mingles about the pack house, chatting about what positions they wish to receive and the lucky ones exclaiming when finding their soulmate, I stick to myself and make my way to a corner of the room where I can be left alone. Most people my age tend to enjoy mingling and talking to one another, but I always felt like an outcast. No one wanted to be friends with the she-wolf that lost her parents and was raised by two male mates. The scent of perfume and cologne is strong with everyone together in such a closed-off space but makes it easier to discern who belongs to which faction. The wolves, standing by the punch bowl most likely spiked with some form of alcohol, who smell like a grade eight locker room where boys use Axe as a shower-in-a-can, are the ones built for power. Each male wolf built with muscle-on-muscle will become a Warrior. Now, they fangirl about some sports game that was on last night and who won.

The group of small wolves that do their best to blend into the background with little to no scent on them will be Omegas, who will do the regular work around the pack, from cooking and cleaning to taking care of the daycare and little kids. These Omegas are what we refer to as the working class since some of them will also help run the companies owned by the pack by doing a nine-to-five job like regular humans. Then there is a group of wolves that fit between the Omegas and Warriors: I call them the Acolytes. They're standing by the bookshelves and seem to be in a heated debate about some type of medical theory. These Acolytes will fill in positions such as Pack Doctors, nurses, architects, builders and any task that requires in-depth and specialized research and planning. We can't rely on humans to help build our community and risk exposing the werewolf race, so these wolves take the place of any jobs that require any university or college degree. If it weren't for my Alpha and Beta bloodline, I would be considered an Acolyte and part of that debate. Taking a seat on an armchair once I reach my destination to the corner with a window I can stare out of, I spot the Alpha talking to a few girls who try their best at looking coy and sexy before him. I always wondered how pushing your body against a male would benefit a she-wolf other than being used and taken advantage of, but I made no comment of their behaviour. I preferred working hard for the things I wanted and being independent. The idea of needing a strong male to take care of and protect me like a precious doll seemed a little old-fashioned to me. It's not that I don't want whoever my mate is, but I crave being independent more. Christ jokes around saying that it's the Alpha blood in me wanting to be respected and not under someone else's control.

Two warriors are standing a respectful distance away from Alpha Sam but close enough to act on his command. These warriors are the ones that will step into action once Alpha Sam designates a she-wolf as the next pack Breeder. They are the wolves everyone fears since they have a higher status than the regular warriors. Not only do they protect the Alpha, but they are also given special privileges as wolves who forsake the mate bond, intending to stay mateless for the rest of their lives just to have their pick of the Breeder populace. At any moment, they can storm into a Breeder's home and fuck her as he pleases. Every mother warns her daughter to never go near the ten warriors dedicated to this position since some abuse their powers to take a she-wolf that catches his eye. There are many stories of she-wolves being raped to please these men when a Breeder is unavailable, and there is nothing the young girl can do other than accept her fate.

I keep an eye on Alpha, knowing that at any moment, he will make his rounds around the room and decide the fate of the newly-shifted. Disgust and annoyance are evident on Alpha's face as a she-wolf gets too close to him, pushing her assets into his face in hopes of seducing Alpha Sam. I blame her behaviour on the many reminders her parents must have given the poor blonde she-wolf before sending her inside the pack house. Most families hope to have their pup mated to the Alpha since this will bring honour and prestige to them. Unfortunately for her, Alpha Sam has never shown any interest in the pack whores let alone a newly-shifted she-wolf like her. Her greed will not get her the position she wants. My turn to speak to him will come soon. I know the two positions I wanted: Acolyte, as I have by-passed high school and am currently enrolled in college, and Warrior, as Chris and Jack have been training me to fight since I was seven years old, and intensified my training once I shifted, to include not only hand-to-hand combat in human form that has been drilled into me for years, but also combat in wolf form.

I turn my attention to the window, deciding to ignore everyone in the room and watch as small pups chase each other around in the yard, their laughter and squeals of delight floating in on the wind through the open window. They look so carefree, and I smile at their game of tag. The scent of summer wildflowers, the dew still clinging to the pack house gardens from this morning, and the fresh aroma of pine surrounding our pack house whisks away the nauseating stench of sweat, perfume and cologne permeating from the wolves in today's meeting in the next hour. I know Chris and Jack want me to mingle with everyone, but I see no point. Many wolves do their best to stay away from me.

Movement from inside the room catches my attention out of the corner of my eye. I turn just in time to watch as Alpha excuses himself from the she-wolves, much to their protest and dismay, and makes his way in my direction, specifically to where I sit in my corner. I smile at our young Alpha Sam, who, at twenty-two, has yet to find his mate to rule beside him as his Luna of this pack. He is the most eligible bachelor who every she-wolf dreams to be mated to and is also why wolves my age steer clear of me.

"Laina, how ni-" He stops mid-greeting, standing before me and sniffing the air, and moves closer to where I sit while he focuses his attention solely on me. Excitement bubbles inside me with the possibility this brings. His scent wafts over me, and a feeling of calmness runs through every nerve ending in my body. *Could I possibly be his mate?*

Sam and I grew up together since my father was once his father's Beta. He used to babysit me during meetings where both of our parents would be busy with pack work. Even if Sam is eight years older than me, as children, he would spend his free time with me, spoiling and treating me to anything my little heart desired. I remember one time he bought me a lacy dark red dress for my twelfth birthday. It was a little revealing for my taste at the time, but I still loved the attention Sam showered me with that day as we took a trip into the city. When each year passed without Sam finding his mate, it gave me some form of hope that maybe I could be his and he mine. Quietly, I wait for his following statement that will decide my fate and role.

"*Breeder.*" His voice is filled with desire as his hands shift to grope my large breasts, a smirk playing at his lips. I gasp in surprise, fear spreading through me with this one word. *This isn't possible, right?*

The two Warriors' stoic faces soon morph into a smirk as their eyes scan me from head to toe. The dark-toned wolf with dreadlocks winks at me as his eyes hold a trace of lust barely visible in his chocolate-coloured gaze. Deep down, I know he will want to take a go at me first. His partner reaches out to grab my left arm as the dreadlock guy takes my right, the grip tight enough to remind me that escape is futile as they will hunt me down. Whispers and sympathetic gazes are sent my way as the two Warriors lead me out of the building. Some she-wolves exclaim in the joy of not being chosen, while others wish me good luck even though I feel far from lucky. I can see some holding their phones, ready to capture a sobbing breakdown that follows each year when a new Breeder is chosen, but I refuse to give these wolves the satisfaction of a good show and instead keep my head held high. I keep my gaze forward and take each step towards the door with as much dignity as I can muster. Never show weakness when forced into an unfavourable situation is what my father used to tell me as a child.

Everyone knows what will happen after you are assigned as a Breeder. You will be whisked away from your family and forced to stay in a cottage guarded day and night, only able to garden in the medium-sized yard given to you. But the truth is, you are nothing but a slave to the warriors assigned to breed you. You will welcome an unknown male into your home, lead him to the bed you sleep in each night, and spread your legs whether you want to or not. You will spend the next six months carefully observed like a rat in a lab while you carry the pup inside you to a healthy delivery, and you will repeat the process a few months later, never given a say as to who will breed you. You are nothing to the pack even after gaining your freedom when the twentieth pup is born. And this is the life I will be living now.

The doors to the pack house close. The pack meeting will proceed as usual now that a new Breeder is chosen. This is when reality begins to sink in. I feel numb, my mind still wrapping around my new role as the men lead me to a black car. The doors are open, waiting to shut me inside and whisk me away from the life I know, but no one forces me into the vehicle. In moments, Chris and Jack will be informed of my position and rush over from whatever it is they are doing, with the prodding eyes of their friends questioning what is wrong, finding me where each Breeder waits for their final words with loved ones. Only a few minutes will be allotted to us, and then I'll be taken away where no one will be able to see me for the next twenty years or so.

Knowing Chris and his obsession with time, they will be here in three...

Two...

One.

Cue a sobbing Chris.

"Laina, are you okay?" Chris's voice fills my ears the moment his arms hold me in a tight hug. I watch as the guards walk away to give us privacy, far enough to not hear a thing but close enough to chase after me if I decide to run. Since this is my last free moment as a regular pack member, the guards are not allowed to listen in, much like giving a prisoner on death row their final meal before taking them to the chair that will end their life. A few minutes of silence fall between us. Chris is sobbing into my shoulder as Jack sends me a grimace of a smile. We all know the situation is dire.

"I...I don't know what to do." I whisper, feeling Jack wipe away stray tears that had fallen from my eyes.

"What you do is behave, wait for a free moment, and run. Run towards the old treehouse, look for something pink, grab it, and keep running." I do not understand what Chris has said, my fuzzy mind unable to comprehend his words before I am ripped away from my best friend and pushed into the car, the door slamming in my face and the engine roaring to life.

I watch in the rearview mirror as my life fades into the distance away from me, the tears now flowing freely.

All I can think of: *Is this how Katniss felt when she was whisked away from her family in District Twelve in The Hunger*

Games?

CHAPTER 2

As the pack territory slowly passes by, I decide to rest my eyes. Breeders are given an area on the far-west side of the territory where no one will be able to disturb them. That area is patrolled and guarded day and night. It will be a community I call home for however long my stay is, but deep down, I know I can never allow the cottage I will be living in to be *my* home. A prison, yes, but never *my home*.

Hope slowly slips away the further I get from the pack house and the closer I get to the cottage where I'll live for the next chapter of my life. At sixteen, I should be enjoying life as a carefree young adult, not being sentenced to life as a mother. I never wanted to raise pups just yet. I had a career in mind that I worked hard towards each and every day, but now it's all gone.

Sighing, I decide to let the comfort of sleep take over. It would be too painful to keep looking out the window and only cause me to break down in front of the men who are probably fighting amongst each other over who will get to use me first after the Alpha does.

Sometime later, I feel the car come to a stop, waking me from the brief moments of slumber in my dreadful situation. The Warriors sitting in the front seats hold a soft conversation barely audible to my wolf hearing, but one thing for sure is that they still think I'm fast asleep and are fighting over who will carry me inside. Deciding that pretending to be asleep is a bad idea for my own safety, I open my tired eyes and take in my surroundings as best as I could within the confines of the vehicle. In front of me is a gorgeous grey brick cottage, with a small porch welcoming me to sit and read during the day. The building had a fairytale look with light blue window trim on the front door and roof and a whimsical aura surrounding it; this is definitely a place I would have loved to live in under any other circumstances. The garden surrounding the cottage clearly needs some TLC to bring out its full potential and beauty, but the white picket fence around the lot's perimeter gave the final touches that this place needs to welcome any newly mated pair. Unfortunately, it will be my new prison, with my own prison guards "protecting" me from now on.

The car door slowly opens, and the guards wait on either side for me to get out. I can't help but sigh in defeat as I climb out of the back seat and step onto the simple dirt driveway. The surrounding area around my new home is the forest I so love to run in. I can't see any other cottages, only the rise of smoke from many chimneys hidden between the tall trees, a clear sign that this area held a few Breeders. Maybe the guards will let me visit them and allow me out of the cottage for a bit every day if I behave well enough for their approval.

I know what is expected of me after I arrive at my new home. From the age of eight, every she-wolf has the Breeder rules drilled into their brains if they became one to prepare us for this position. Each new Breeder is given three days to explore the house and design it in a way the Breeder deems suitable for comfortable living, including painting any and all walls, decorating the interior to her preference and performing some landscaping in the front and back gardens. On the fourth day of being in the cottage, the Doctor assigned to take care of all Breeders will come to do a check-up and make sure the Breeder is healthy, with the Alpha in tow. If the Breeder is a virgin, it is the Alpha's duty to take matters into his own hands by fucking the Breeder as much as he wants on that day. Thank god the Alpha will be using a condom as per the rules since I've heard that once a Breeder is selected, the she-wolf's body will change to accommodate the new role and will be able to fall pregnant very easily. At least, that is what the rumours are. After that, the Breeder is given three days to be pampered and prescribed a dose of medication that they are expected to take to make sure her body is ready to start their new "job." On the eighth day after arriving, the top mateless Warrior is sent to the cottage and will come every day to fuck her like a cheap whore until she becomes pregnant. This is the new life I have been thrown into without concern for my own well-being. The Warrior who is chosen to breed me will continue this process as my designated partner and continue to make me produce his pups until he finds his mate. Then I will be given a new breeding partner, and the cycle repeats until I birth twenty pups.

Of course, there are exceptions. Warriors who choose to never find their mate are given the chance to pick any Breeder they want whenever they want and are allowed to fuck them as much as they want. They were the ones many she-wolves avoid on a regular day. But, as a Breeder, all I can do is spread my legs and allow them to do as they please without being able to fight against their advances, swallow with a smile and thank them for their time. The sad part about this is once the pups are weaned, they will be taken to wolves that can't have pups and be raised by these wolves as if they were born to that mated pair. I will never be able to be a mother to my own children.

After fighting back the emotions wanting to surface since being designated as the next Breeder, I fall to my knees. This is real, I am a Breeder, and I will never know my babies once they are taken away from me. I am nothing but a baby-making machine now to this pack. The guards must have felt some form of sympathy for me because they back away and leave me to myself, something I am thankful for even though just moments ago they were fighting about who will fuck me first. My dream of building my career, finding my mate, and raising a family is now lost in oblivion, scattered on the winds of pain that seem to course through my breaking heart. I will never have my freedom ever again.

Soon my cries morph into sobs, wailing until I am left gasping for breath. I want to run far away and escape my fate, but I can't. I would be caught in a heartbeat and punished. So instead, I dry my eyes as best as I can and stand up, determination pulsating in my veins. I march into the cottage, turn around and stop the guards from entering.

"This is my house now! The only time I have no say in who comes in is when the Alpha or the Warrior who will breed with me comes in. Other than that, you two stay outside." They growl at my disrespectful behaviour, and I growl back just as loudly. I may have had a moment of weakness earlier, but I'll be damned if they disrespect me. I may be a Breeder now, but Alpha and Beta blood courses through my body thanks to my parents. No one will take my courage and the status of my bloodline away from me.

Watching the warriors bend to my growl and back away, I give them a triumphant smirk before slamming the door shut. I will allow no one into this place unless it is the Alpha, the Doctor, my breeding partner or someone I trust. Turning around and leaning against the blue door, I notice how dusty the place is and frown. The first thing to be done is cleaning from top to bottom. I refuse to live in a dirty, dusty home. I quickly explore the cottage, finding a large room with cleaning supplies that looked to be a laundry room with a state-of-the-art washer and dryer waiting to be used. The idiots in charge of maintaining the Breeder cottages remembered to stock up on cleaning supplies but forgot to clean the place.

I smile sadly and leave the cleaning supplies where they are to continue exploring the other rooms. The rest of the cottage has a new modern kitchen with a fully stocked refrigerator and pantry, three plain bedrooms, a master bedroom with an ensuite bath, and a small bathroom in the second-floor hallway intended for others to use. I am actually quite shocked to see how big the cottage actually is inside, but sad that there is no basement. It would have been nice to turn the basement into a workout room. Making my way back towards the laundry room, I come to another door just beside the entranceway and peek inside, shocked to find a garage. I guess the wall covered in vines on the outside is actually the garage door. With a smile, I decide to turn this into my home gym. I would need some place to keep me in shape if I am to have multiple children.

Getting to work, I run through the two-story cottage once again, searching through all the closets to find linen, bedspreads, towels, and any other textiles that would need to be cleaned. After a few trips, I soon had everything gathered in the laundry room, sorted into multiple baskets, with a load already in the wash. I had a lot of work to be done.

With the laundry started, I begin to rush around once more, opening all the windows and the glass door to the backyard to allow fresh air to blow inside while I start cleaning. I knew the clothes I am wearing would be ruined, but I would rather have a clean prison than clean clothes right now. I can always change later when my clothes are sent to me. I hated knowing that I only had three days to clean and prepare my new home. With determination, I make a promise to myself that no matter how late I get to a bed today, I will make sure this place is clean and dust-free. It sucks, but the cleaning must be done.

CHAPTER 3

I look at my handiwork in the kitchen. This is the last room to be cleaned. All the dishes are now done and stored nicely and neatly in the cupboards. It has been an exhausting day, from being designated as the new Breeder to my small breakdown outside and finally having to clean an entire cottage all by myself. I should have made a stupid guard help me clean since their job is to basically keep me locked in this property. Still, the thought of one of the wolves outside stepping into my designated space causes the anger to swell inside me at this unjust situation.

I lean against the marble counter, a glass of red wine from the bottle I found in the pantry in my hands. Taking a sip, I turn to look at the time on the microwave—ten o'clock at night. I know that as a sixteen-year-old, I'm three years underage to legally drink in Canada but fuck it, I really need something strong after the day I've had. Chris always limited me to one glass of wine at functions, so the alcohol has little effect on me. Suddenly, something vibrates against my leg, causing me to jump and nearly choke on my drink. Remembering that I had stashed my cellphone into the pocket of my skirt earlier this morning, I place the glass on the counter and proceed to take out the device. My screen flashes with a picture of me and my best friend Abby, and a small smile plays on my lips as I slide my finger across the screen to answer her incoming call. "Hey, Ab-" I begin, heading upstairs as she cuts my greeting off.

"Is it true? Are you the newest Breeder?" I wince at her words and sigh—something I've been doing all day—telling her to give me a moment since there are guards outside my cottage. Heading towards the master bedroom, I make my way towards the bath and turn on the shower, letting the running water mask our conversation.

"Yeah, it's true, sadly," I reply after a while, sliding down the wall to sit on the cold tiled floor.   "We have to save you!" My best friend exclaims, worry evident in her voice. The tears start to pool in my blue eyes and escape down my cheeks.

"You can't do anything. Think about your mate. He's the Beta here, and if Alpha Sam finds out you tried to free me, imagine what would happen." My voice cracks as I begin to sob again for the second time today. I make a quick decision and tell my best friend all my fears and worries about my new position, about how I wish I wasn't chosen as a Breeder at all and wish I had met my mate before today since mated females are safe from becoming a Breeder. By the end of my sobbing rant, I feel better with a clearer mind. Talking to a friend really helps.

"I know I'm allowed to come to see you tomorrow to help get the house decorated, so I'll bring you some essentials. What do you want?" Abby says quietly, trying to distract me from the current situation. I smile and let out a chuckle at her antics. As the Beta Female and surrogate Luna of this pack, my friend has a say in what happens with the new Breeder, and it is her job to help the Breeder settle in on the second day. I somehow got lucky, with Abby being my best friend and growing up together as children, even if she is three years older than me.

"As many clothes as you can grab from my closet, lots of chocolate to help my emotionally unstable mind right now and my phone charger, please. Talk to my cousin and his mate about stuff to bring for me." I rattle off a list, glad that my friend's status allows her to visit me whenever she wants.

"Okay, I will see you tomorrow then." She reassures me as we say our good nights and end our phone call. I turn off all sound on my phone, not wanting the guards to take it away from me in case I need to reach Chris or Jack in an emergency. I turn off the shower, and silence resumes. Trying to think of a hiding spot in my room where no one will find my cellphone, I leave the bathroom and make my way towards the nightstand beside the bed and pull open the top drawer, a wide grin spread across my face. What looks to be a simple empty drawer actually holds a pleasant surprise: a false bottom that I had discovered in my mad cleaning session. It was something I guess the previous Breeder had created using a piece of wood matching the nightstand since she had left a leather notebook containing what I assume to be a biography or note for the next Breeder now sitting on the nightstand. I plan to read it at some point to see just how the Breeder who once resided here lived daily. Hopefully, this book could give me details on how to survive and what I can do to make my life less miserable as a Breeder.

Once my cellphone is secure in its hiding spot, I look at the leather notebook and debate whether I should read it or not. Curiosity wins out as I grab it with one hand and sit cross-legged in the middle of the bed, taking the time to read what my predecessor wrote. I decide that reading everything in one sitting is a bad idea and focus on the first few pages. I quickly discovered that this notebook is actually a diary. My focus is captivated by the first entry from twenty years ago when she was forced to become a Breeder and what transpired on that day. My heart breaks for this she-wolf who remains nameless in her entry, as she wrote about being immediately dragged away to the cottage without a goodbye to her family. She was thrown into this cottage that was completely empty compared to what it is now— save for a bed—and this she-wolf spent her night cold and lonely. I felt better knowing that the treatment this she-wolf went through is different from what I went through today. At least I had some food in the fridge, and there is some form of furniture and bedding for me to use, even if the other rooms were empty.

Taking the time to read the next entry, my eyes widen in horror. Instead of the she-wolf having a few days to settle into her new role, the breeding process started the next morning. She had lost all her rights as a regular wolf right away. My heart drops in horror as I read of her being awoken and promptly raped by the Alpha and another Warrior. There was neither the courtesy that we experience now nor any humane treatment.

Placing the leather book down, I take a deep breath and re-evaluate my situation. I could settle into my new role, knowing I have a few days to take everything in and focus on any plan I could, or I could fight back and possibly be injured. I decided a shower would do me well with the new information from the diary and make my way to the bathroom, turn the shower on and undress while the water comes to a temperature I prefer. Stepping into the spray of warm water, I allow my thoughts to circulate with the rules I was told of being a Breeder, what the next few days will be like for me as well as the two entries from the Diary. If I want to survive, I will have to be obedient as a Breeder for now and do what I am told. Accepting my fate, I pick up the loofa and scrub away the grime from cleaning off of my body. My mind wanders to the thought of what to do with this cottage. I think of what to do with the other rooms since I have no choice but to perform this role as the pack's Breeder. Since I would need a nursery for the many newborns, I will be forced to have and a room for any toddlers, I would have to decorate those rooms first. The time ticks by, and I force myself to stop thinking. Anything that needs to be done can be dealt with tomorrow.

With the water turning cold, I turn off the water and step out of the shower, wrapping my body in a towel that envelops my small body. I slowly open the bathroom door, the steam escaping the warm room. I start to shiver from the cold breeze that rushes to greet me. Quickly, I run to the walk-in closet, taking the oversized, long-sleeved shirt and boy shorts I had found and cleaned earlier and quickly towel-dried my body to put the fresh set of clothes on.

Padding quietly into my room, I shiver once again, remembering that all the windows were opened when I began cleaning earlier. I want nothing more than to fall into the queen-sized mattress and allow sleep to take over. But instead, I rush around the cottage, closing all the windows and the back door. Even though it is late spring now, the weather in our pack territory still held up as early-spring-almost-at-the-end-of-winter weather since we are located in the northern part of Ontario, close to the Hudson Bay. Checking the thermostat to make sure the cottage warms up, I finally head back upstairs and into my room. I climb into bed, wrapping the warm, soft blankets around me and letting my exhausted body relax as the scent of the lavender fabric softener surrounds and soothes me into a deep, dreamless sleep.

CHAPTER 4

Early in the morning, I wake up with sleep-filled eyes, taking in the blurry surroundings. For a moment, I panic, thinking that I am in the wrong house. Before long, the events of the previous day flood into my mind.

Taking deep, calming breaths, I push the covers off of me and stand, taking a big stretch. I head into the bathroom to comb my hair into a messy bun that sits atop my head, wash my face, brush my teeth, and finally relieve my bladder. Today, Abby will arrive with my belongings.

Sighing yet again, I stumble out of my bedroom and make my way downstairs into the kitchen. I take out some ingredients for my classic comfort food—banana-chocolate chip pancakes. I figure Abby would want to eat with me, and, boy, can that girl pack down food like it's nothing! So, I triple my usual recipe.

As soon as the pancakes are done and the stovetop is turned off, I hear the doorbell ring with a visitor's arrival; I make my way over to the front of the house, opening the blue wooden door to see Abby standing there accompanied by four Warriors. The giant, burly Warriors are each holding a bag and boxes with "Laina's stuff" written on them in black Sharpie.

"Morning, girl. Do I smell.. pancakes?" Abby grins as she pulls me in for a long hug. The Warriors head inside, taking my things up the stairs. I tell them to leave everything in the master bedroom before ordering them all to leave.

As soon as they leave, Abby winks and holds a tote bag out to me. I can't help the grateful smile I send her way as I take the bag and look inside, happy to see my phone charger, wallet, and other essentials that a Breeder isn't allowed to have. I'm so happy that my friend snuck these in for me.

"Thank you, Abby," I whisper. The two of us head into the kitchen, where a heaping stack of pancakes awaits us. We gather some plates and utensils and begin to dig into the scrumptious breakfast and catch up. Abby goes on about the gossip around the pack, thankfully steering clear of mentioning any rumours about me. It felt normal to be in the kitchen with my best friend, scarfing down comfort food and chatting like regular teenagers.

Abby offers to clear the table and load the dishwasher while I head upstairs to get changed. Looking through the boxes and bags in my room, I manage to find a pair of leggings and a comfy cropped hoodie to wear with black sneakers and my purse. Fully dressed, I make my way to the foot of the stairs, where Abby waits to head out. Today will be spent shopping for this house, and the first stop is the home gym equipment. I would save the baby stuff for last... For now.

...

"That's all for shopping," Abby exclaims. We left the cottage around eleven in the morning to make it to the nearest mall. Our first stop had been the sports store, where I hunted down some equipment to turn the garage into a home gym. Abby thought that I had gone absolutely insane for wanting to create a home workout area, but when I pointed out I would need to stay in shape for my job, she quieted down and agreed with me. Every store we went to offers delivery to the pack house and will deliver my purchases to my cottage tomorrow. Despite the thrill of shopping, it makes me sad thinking that the first house I'll ever decorate is the prison of the Breeder's cottage.

"Now, it's time to get home to all the paint waiting for you to paint each wall." I can tell Abby is trying to stay cheerful, but her words are really starting to annoy me. She sounds more formal than friendly. I know my job as a Breeder means that Abby would have a say in what I will have to do as the Beta Female of the pack, and smiling around her soon becomes harder. It felt like each sentence she said throughout the day became more and more insensitive. At one point, she told me, "Just choose a damned crib and let's go!" seemingly because it wouldn't matter what I chose anyway. The baby will be whisked away from me as soon as they're able to eat baby food. I guess my mood must have shown; Abby rolls her eyes at me while we climb into her car.

"It's going to be fine. Besides, I hear that Max is your first Warrior, and knowing him, he won't do anything with you. He's saving himself for when he finds his mate." Now, Abby's words do reassure me to some degree. Everyone knows that Max is an honest wolf. He grew up with the notion of "saving himself" for his mate, and, to this day, he's still a virgin. Part of me hopes he doesn't find his mate until I figure out what to do, but maybe, just maybe, I might be his mate. The only hope of getting me out of this situation is if one of the Warriors meant to breed with me is my mate.

"Thank god for that," I grumble a half-hearted reply, looking out at the scenery flashing by. Abby laughs at my words while she turns up the radio volume, singing along to whatever song is playing. I don't feel like joining her; her mood is a little too happy while she takes me back to the baby-making prison, I will be stuck in. I hate this.

Soon, her Land Rover crosses our back borders, and the familiar houses and forest pass by. The road to the breeder section greets us, and my cottage comes into view. Part of me wants to run away at this moment, but the consequences would be dire. As Abby pulls into the driveway, I feel the dread settle in even more. The situation is becoming all the more real and hopeless than ever right now.

"Well, where would you like to paint first?" Abby asks, shutting off the engine and turning off the racket coming from the radio, enveloping us in silence.

"The nursery. I want to paint it powder blue." I answer. It will never be the design I want for my babies because it will never be theirs for the rest of their lives, and I will never raise them and watch them grow up. A trail of warmth flows down my face, and I reach up, feeling fresh tears on my skin. I don't think I could do this at all.

"Laina, are you okay? Seriously, you need to pull yourself together because you're a fucking Breeder, and it's your job. Get used to this and stop crying." Abby gives me a sideways glance, with a look of utter scorn and annoyance on her face. I stare at my so-called best friend in disbelief for a moment, about to challenge her vicious glare. *Is this how she really feels about all of this, considering I'm supposed to be her best friend?*

"Does it look like I'm okay, Abby? Does it look like I'm used to this fucking situation already? My life got turned upside-fucking-down yesterday, and you're telling me to get used to it?!" I shout, my voice shaking. I've finally snapped at her. I can't believe how insensitive she is being right now, this last statement from her being the proverbial straw that broke the camel's back after all her snarky comments from our day-long shopping trip.

I start to rant. "You get to live a happy fucking life with a mate who loves you, and you get to have pups that YOU will raise," I scream, the volume blocking her from saying anything while I slam my fist into her stupid Land Rover's dashboard. It dents with my strength from my rage.

My fists feel like they're burning. "Do you want to know how long my pups will be in my life? Two fucking years. That's it!" I continue, feeling the tears flow faster.

The fury takes over my thoughts. "I don't get to be the mother my pups deserve. I don't get to see their first steps or first words. Their first day of school will be with their adoptive family, who rips my children from my arms to raise them. I get nothing, and all you can do is help me get this place ready for me to be raped in and tell me to get used to my job." I can feel the anger radiating off my friend, but I allow the power in my blood to radiate off of me in waves to cover her, watching her cower before me. I know Abby envies my bloodline having Alpha and Beta blood. She knows full well that her heritage is that of a Breeder's pup with an unknown father and hates her bloodline even though the wolves who raised her treated her like a princess. I guess she likes knowing my so-called "perfect life" she always made comments about came to an end now that I am a Breeder. I would be at her beck and call with her position as the Beta Female. I never noticed how much of a snake Abby is until today, and I start questioning her real motives for being my friend. I start questioning everything she has ever said or done while being a part of my life.

"Geez, Laina, tell me how you really feel?" Her sarcastic remark and glaring eyes filled with hatred simmering in waves towards my direction cause a low warning-growl to escape my lips. She may be a Beta Female and I but a lowly Breeder and inferior in comparison, but she knows I could have her head with my strength at any given moment. At the end of the day, my bloodline is superior to hers.

"Stay out of my life from now on," I reply as I violently push open the car door to get out and slam it shut. I hear the sound of the metal grinding together, knowing that the car door will never open again. *I guess this bitch will need a new car.* I make my way into the house as the squeal of tires fills my ears, knowing that Abby is running away both in fear and humiliation. She could never handle having someone yell at her the way I just did and was probably on her way to complain to her mate.

"Miss Laina?" One of the guards calls out to me while I try to calm the anger and indignation swirling inside me. I smile meekly at his worry-filled gaze, hoping that he doesn't see through my thoughts.

"Don't worry about it," I whisper, and he nods unconvinced before handing me a handkerchief.

"My mother was a Breeder. I knew that the people who raised me weren't my real parents. It just didn't feel right. One day, while we were school shopping, a woman came up to me and said my name. Everything about her seemed so familiar, and the next thing I knew, I was hugging her and begging her not to leave me. My adoptive parents finally told me who she was that night, and after that, I met my siblings. My mother and I still talk to this day, not the one who raised me, but the woman who was forced to give me up—though I still talk to my adoptive parents. I know what your children will go through. Just remember that if I can find a way to get you out before it's too late, I will." My eyes widen at the guard's confession, and I hug him without thinking. Part of me instantly feels safe with this guard, and I can't help but show weakness in front of him, something I hate showing but have been doing lately. His past is similar to Abby, but while she shows her true colours like a royal spoiled bitch, even when her adoptive parents did their best to give her every-thing she wanted, this guard shows sincerity and friendship. The wolves who raised him did well in raising this wolf who stands before me into a well-mannered man.

"I'm Alex, by the way." He laughs out loud, reassuringly patting my back.

"Well, Alex, I'm recruiting you to paint the rooms with me." We laugh together as I release Alex from my hug, motion-ing for the Warrior to follow me inside, where cans of paint are waiting to be used up. I wipe my tears finally and roll up my sleeves. For the rest of the day, we spent the hours painting each room. Alex is a great help, with him being so tall and able to reach the top of the ceiling. It felt nice doing something mun-dane and not being looked at like a piece of meat that the other guards want to take a bite out of.

The next day, Alex arrives early, just in time for the break-fast I made for the two of us before we get to work. I let him know that the furniture will arrive today and ask if he knows anyone he trusts who would be willing to help bring it to the cottage and move it around.

Soon, I meet his half-brother Matthew, a dark-skinned wolf with a carefree smile. He, too, is a Warrior, and I learn that the two of them have been secretly helping Breeders escape when the chance is given to them. Hope flashes briefly in my heart when they agree to help me out when the opportunity arises. Matthew brought along his mate, Milly, to help decorate with a woman's touch. Neither of them brought up the fact that I'm the newest Breeder. They treat me with respect, and it feels nice being treated as an equal and not a slave used to increase the population. Of course, once all the furniture is arranged and built and the walls painted, Alex and Matthew escape into the garage's home gym for a good workout. Milly and I are left to roll our eyes at them and spend the evening with wine and snacks. The only thing that surprised the two wolf-brothers is me being sixteen, apparently, the youngest she-wolf to be chosen as a Breeder.

"You know, it's been fun hanging out with you," Alex says, the two of us sitting on the back porch with hot cocoa in our hands. Matthew and Milly had left about three hours ago, leaving the cottage to feel slightly empty without their presence and laughter.

"It's been fun hanging with you too." I laugh, a genuine smile on my face. Part of me envies Alex's mate, whoever she or he might be, as Alex really is an outstanding wolf. Being mateless, Alex always talks about his hope of finding his mate and spending the rest of their lives together. I know he will make some wolf happy one day, and I hope that day comes soon for him.

"Well, I should let you go rest. The Alpha comes to check on you tomorrow." He kisses the top of my head gently and heads inside. I can hear the sink running as he cleans his mug and calls out his goodbye. Soon enough, he is gone for the night.

Sighing, I head inside and start getting ready for bed, taking a shower and making sure everything is ready for tomorrow. Whether I like it or not, the Alpha will take my virginity tomorrow, and I will fully become a Breeder. Four days after tomorrow, my job will begin, and the first Warrior to be my partner will show up and do what he has to do to make me pregnant. Dread fills me as I try my best to fall asleep, but if Abby was correct the other day, Max will not touch me.

CHAPTER 5

I turn off the tap to the sink as I finish cleaning the dishes from breakfast. Alex sends a sad smile in my direction before quietly leaving the cottage to patrol the perimeter. No one else is allowed to be in the cottage after ten in the morning until the Alpha and the Doctor arrive to conduct their business. The Alpha will stay all night to do with me as he pleases and prepare me for my new role. Anxiety and nerves take over as I wring out the dish towel, trying to find something to do other than smoothing out the non-existent wrinkles in my outfit.

I'm dressed in a simple white lace dress with a matching bra and thong, something one of the guards told me to wear, considering I am still pure, still a virgin. It scares me to think that today Alpha Sam will take away something I wanted to save for my mate, without a care in the world and without any consideration for my well-being; this will be nothing at all like the Sam I grew up with.

Another hour passes. I find some things to clean in the spotless cottage, trying to distract myself from the inevitable that is soon to come. I started thinking that maybe the Alpha had forgotten about today and his job of taking away my virginity, but my hopes are soon crushed when the front door swings open and he and the Doctor waltz in.

"Good morning Miss Laina. Hope you are doing well." Doctor Freelan greets me, his eyes roaming my body. I suppress a shudder and smile as sweetly as I can, bowing my head in submission. As a Breeder, I have to be good and obey these two males or risk being punished each time I disobey them on their visits. I once saw a Breeder be punished about two years ago. Apparently, she tried running away from her role, only to be caught. The Warriors in charge of guarding her took a silver whip—silver being our Kryptonite—while another set of Warriors tied her hands to a pole. The attempted escape happened two days after being assigned her new role. The guards took turns raising the whip and lowering the ends onto her back as I watched on in horror as the silver tips shredded the fair and delicate skin, and blood dripped down her body to pool onto the dirt floor below her. No one knew what happened to this Breeder but the memory of her screams and pleads for mercy on that day reminded me that Breeders are nothing but slaves. Now, as a Breeder myself, I will have to bide my time if I want to survive with the possibility of escape.

"Good morning, Doctor, Alpha." I greet politely, welcoming the two into the living room as if the thought of escape never crossed my mind. The Doctor wastes no time after initial greetings, and the morning passes quickly. I am tested, weighed, measured, and had blood and urine samples taken for the Doctors at the Pack Hospital labs to do tests on. Doctor Freelan leaves with his bag full of notes on my health and the vials to be tested, leaving Alpha Sam and myself alone in the cottage. Nerves once again take over me, and I excuse myself to hide away in the kitchen to cook. It would be unwise to deal with a hungry Alpha, and this task gave me something to keep my nerves at bay. After a quick lunch with Alpha Sam, Doctor Freelan returns with a beaming smile and joins Alpha and I at the dining room table.

"You're fit and strong. Your pups will be amazing." He announces with delight. I groan internally while my outer appearance displays a grateful expression. *Never show weakness to those you consider your enemy.*

"Thank you so much," I reply, faking a relieved breath, getting ready to kick the Doctor out of my cottage. It will be quicker to get the deed over with and done and allow the Alpha to take my virginity away now without any fight.

"I am not done yet." Doctor Freelan continues, making it hard for me to hold in the sigh of irritation that builds with each moment the Doctor stays in this cottage. I jump when Alpha Sam clears his throat, forcing me to turn my body in his direction to give the wolf my full attention.

"As you know, since becoming Alpha six years ago, I haven't found my mate, and I need an heir by this time next year. Otherwise, my brother and his mate will take over as Alpha and Luna." I nod with confusion, not understanding where this conversation is going.

"The pack Elders and I have decided that the first pup you will bear will be my own. If you can produce two pups for me, then your position as a Breeder will be nullified, and you can become a female Warrior or Acolyte. The choice is yours." *This offer feels too good to be true but at what cost? Would his mate even accept his pups from a Breeder?*

A moment of silence settles between all of us as I take a moment to think. I could weigh the pros and cons of this offer all day if I wanted, but I had a feeling they would want me to answer now. Finally resigning to my fate, I look at the Alpha and give him a small smile.

"Do I even have a choice?" I ask in a small voice, already knowing his answer.

"No." Both men say in unison. I sigh, turning to look at the Doctor.

"So what role do you play?" I ask, watching a sadistic grin spread across his wrinkle-filled face.

"This one!" He exclaims happily, opening his bag and producing a needle with the point gleaming evilly in the light. A liquid sloshes around in the glass tube, the amber colour sending a sense of foreboding through me. I had a feeling I would not like what he is about to do.

Before I can comprehend what is happening, the Alpha has his hands on my arms, holding me in place as the Doctor moves quickly, shoving the point of the needle into my left arm with such accuracy that I feel he has done this hundreds of times already. A tingling sensation courses through my body as the Doctor slowly removes the needle after making sure every last fluid in the syringe is injected into my body. I want to feel fear or the urge to fight my way out of their grasps, but none comes. Only shock fills me with what these men have done.

"You have a week to get her pregnant with this serum. Her sex drive will be hyperactive, and it will feel like she is in heat, so have fun." Doctor Freelan gathers his things after these instructions and leaves my cottage. My skin slowly blooms with a slight blush as I begin to pant for air. The room begins to feel hot and humid on my sensitive skin, and the Alpha grazes his fingertips across my arms, causing me to let out a loud sensual moan.

"Guess it's starting to work..." The Alpha's smug voice fills the room, and I feel myself being lifted into his strong arms as he forces me to straddle his lap. I watch as his lips descend onto my neck, sending torturous kisses and nips on my now-sensitive skin, causing the valley between my legs to drip with wetness. I gasp as his lips find a sweet spot just on the swell of my breasts, his kisses moving the clothes aside as he exposes the hard bud of my nipple. He sucks my nipple into his mouth, causing me to moan and grind myself against the bulge in his pants.

"This is going to be fun, Miss Laina." He growls. His lips smash onto my own, and his hands cup my ass as he stands from the chair, my legs instinctively wrapping around his waist. I could feel him moving towards the stairs. Moments later, I find myself being lowered onto my bed, the Alpha on top of me and between my legs. I feel him slowly grinding himself into the thin material of the lacy white thong that I know is just soaking wet with my juices.

"Alpha!" I whimper. Everything in me knows this is wrong. This is not supposed to happen. But the primal instinct of my wolf side wants nothing more than to be mounted and pounded into by the man above me.

"Call me Sam, baby girl." Sam's husky voice fills my ears as his strong hands tear my dress apart, leaving me in nothing but the push-up bra and soaking thong. His lips once again descend onto my skin, kissing, sucking, biting me, causing me to grind harder into him and moan. My body is burning with desire by now. The drug injected into me is doing its job as Sam rips my bra away. He wraps his lips around the hard rosy nipple, sucking and biting hard on it. His callous fingers find their way past the thong and into my pussy, slowly stretching me and moving against the wet flesh. Pressure soon begins to build inside me; my moans and screams fill the room as I clutch at my bed sheets, my hips moving in sync with Sam's fingers deep inside me. Finally, my insides clench, contracting against the three digits that Sam manages to squeeze inside as liquid oozes out and onto my thigh. I gasp for air, but the feeling of wanting more fills my mind as I hazily look up at the smirking male before me.

"Now that you've had your first orgasm, I want to feel your pretty little mouth wrapped around me for a moment." Sam orders, his hand, still wet with my juices, leaving me as he undresses to reveal a well-built and muscular body for my eyes to feast. I gulp when I catch sight of his hard, thick cock ready to be plunged inside me. He reaches for my head and wraps his fingers in my chestnut locks, pulling my head forwards until my lips brush against the tip of him.

"Open up and suck, bitch." He orders. My mouth opens upon his Alpha command and he quickly pushes his length inside me, causing me to groan. My pussy still twitches, wanting more pleasure, but I have to do what I am told. One hand reaches out to steady my body on the bed while the other grasps the base of Sam's cock, moaning as I begin to suck and caress my tongue against him. I watch as he grunts and groans with pleasure, his eyes glazing over as he rhythmically thrusts into my mouth. Sometimes he would hit the back of my throat, causing me to gag on him, which only encourages Sam to continue that movement over and over again. He pushes me back out of nowhere.

"I'm close to coming, Laina, and I am far from done with you." Sam forces me onto my back and spreads my legs, positioning himself just at my entrance and rubbing the tip of his penis just against my wet folds before pushing into me without warning. I cry out from the pain of his rod penetrating my hymen and taking away my virginity. He thrusts hard and fast inside me. Soon, pleasure takes over pain as he wraps his hand around my throat. The hours pass, and I scream in both excruciating pain and the most blissful pleasure, feeling his muscular, sweaty, naked body on top of mine while he plunges into me. Sometimes he would flip me onto my hands and knees, taking me from behind and smacking my ass or yanking my hair, calling me his filthy whore, his girl, as I let him take my body any way he pleases. At some point, I lost all senses, only able to feel the wolf inside me, begging for more. Finally, we finish, and I lay pressed to his side, panting, him still inside me as his seed continues to flow inside for the ninth time tonight.

"Soon, you will give me an heir." He whispers, his hand rubbing my back.

My mind is screaming. This is still wrong. This is against the rules. But my body craves for more. I curse whatever the Doctor injected into me.

For the next week, with each time the Alpha visited, my body always craves him the moment he steps inside the door. My bedroom begins to hold a permanent scent of sex and sweat. I lost count of how many times Sam came inside me. It is ludicrous, but it is my job now, and I have to do what I am told or else I would end up with torn flesh like the Breeder from two years ago.

My job now is to produce heirs for Sam.

CHAPTER 6

Today is a week from when Alpha Sam had started coming to the cottage.

I stare at the small stick in my hand. I begin to cry, not because I am happy, but because my life has taken a sharp one-eighty turn with no end in sight. It will be six months until this pup is born. That's how long a she-wolf is pregnant. There will be two years until Alpha takes away the wolf inside me and raises his heir without me in this pup's life.

"Laina?" Alex's voice floats through the door and I jump, flushing the toilet and throwing the evidence of my pregnancy away in the trash bin. I do not want anyone to find out that I'm pregnant right away. Hell, part of me is ashamed for how I acted over the last week with the Alpha. I curse the Doctor each time I am left alone in bed, as the Alpha leaves my used and bruised body that he has just filled with his seed for the umpteenth time to do pack work before returning to make me his own little sex toy once more. Washing my face with cold water, I compose myself and force from my mind the thoughts of what I was forced to do for the past seven days, then leave the safety of the master bathroom.

"You okay?" Alex asks as I walk past him.

"Yeah, I'm just overwhelmed." I smile as best as I can at my friend and usher him out of the room. "I'll see you in a few, just want to tidy up." My friend nods and closes the door giving me a moment to myself.

I have to focus on putting together a bag of things I will

need if I want to run away soon. Alex and Matthew will help me if I tell them about what Doctor Freelan and Alpha Sam did to me. Grabbing a small pink notebook, I take out my hidden phone, writing down all important contacts before I start making a list of things I will need as well. I will have to leave my cell phone behind or risk being tracked by Sam and his Warriors.

With the drug out of my system now, my mind feels much clearer and refreshed than it has in days. Today is my best option for running away since Alpha is gone for the whole day due to pack business and will only return tonight with Doctor Freelan to give me a check-up. It is now or never, and part of me continues to hold on to the hope that Alex and Matthew will help me like Breeders before when I inform them of my plan to escape.

I smile at the one good thing Abby has done to help me, her bringing my emergency money and wallet with all my cards and I.D. inside. I haven't heard from or seen that bitch since she left me here, but Milly said she has been gloating about the mighty Laina Starcrest becoming nothing but a fuck toy. I'm glad I dropped her as a friend when I did; who knows what she would have done if I allowed her to continue coming to this cottage. I stuff my wallet into a large duffle bag I kept by the bed and begin to rummage around the room, picking and choosing what would be essential to bring with me, including practical clothing and an extra pair of running shoes.

With the duffle bag packed and leaving enough room for other things like food, water, and medical supplies, I slowly open the door to the bedroom and heighten my wolf hearing, taking the time to see if Alex is in the house. He isn't, thank the Goddess.

I smile before making my way downstairs and into the kitchen, grabbing a handful of protein and granola bars and several bags of jerky and dried fruit and throwing them all into the bag with my stuff. I then make my way towards where the first aid kit is kept under the kitchen sink. I choose what I will most likely need on the run, placing bandages, gauze, medical tape, pain medication and disinfectant spray into a large Ziploc bag, making sure everything is secured in the bag. I rush outside to hide the duffle bag by the back gate.

Today will be my great escape, and I have a feeling that this will be the number-one gossip in the pack when I leave. I just have to plan when to run during the shift change for the guards.

Smiling triumphantly, I turn towards the cottage and take in the building and its surroundings. This place will never be my home if I have a say in it, but for now, I need to act as if it's just another day. After making sure the bag I've hidden won't be seen, I make my way back inside and head straight for the kitchen. I need to eat something filling today and decide on some comfort food—lasagna sounds like a good idea. I busy myself preparing the Italian dish, making sure each layer has enough meat and cheese with a little bit of sauce, before placing it in the oven to bake. As a last-minute addition, I add a baking sheet with some garlic bread alongside the lasagna. Meat and carbs are a werewolf's best friend when planning to run any distance, whether for training or running away.

"Food smells good," Alex says as he enters the kitchen from the back door. A plateful of cookies and another with sliced garlic bread were already on the table, ready to be devoured. I bring the hot lasagna out of the oven and settle the tray between the two plates.

"Yeah, come on and dig in." I laugh at my friend's enthusiasm for food.

[Laina, the Doctor and I can't come over today, we have urgent pack business at the pack house. Stay inside!]

The Alpha's voice rings clear in my head as he links me with a hint of urgency in his voice. I sigh in relief and sit down at the table, digging into my food, my mood becoming lighter.

With this information, the check-up seems to be cancelled, and I can't help but grin. My chance for escape increases, knowing that the two males who have made my life a nightmare for the last seven days will not make an appearance tonight. If the check-up had gone as scheduled and if I weren't pregnant, I would have most likely been dosed with the serum again and repeated the process with the Alpha once more. Luckily, neither of those options will happen. But a nagging feeling fills me. Why would the Alpha still be on pack lands when he had gone out this morning?

"Good news?" Alex asks. I nod, giving him a full smile as I shove a fork full of delicious pasta into my mouth.

"He isn't coming today, neither is the Doctor," I mumble through a mouthful of garlic bread, catching sight of Alex as he lets out a relieved sigh and his body relaxes.

"Good. As taboo as it is to say, I hate the Alpha." He says. I laugh, almost choking on my food. I love how honest my friend is with me.

"Don't worry, I hate the Alpha too!" We continue our lunch, the mood lighter with the knowledge Alpha Sam and Doctor Freelan will not be making an appearance today, giving us time to catch up. I hesitate to tell Alex my plan, knowing that even though he has helped other Breeders escape this fate, I am a special case. I carry Pine Paw's heir now.

"Alex, we have a problem!" James, the other guard in charge of keeping me prisoner to this cottage, shouts. I can hear not-so-distant growls and howls.

"Rogues," Alex says hurriedly as his body tenses, ready to fight. He rushes over to the back door and looks outside before coming back to my side with hope in his eyes, hope that ignites the fighting spirit inside of me.

"Our job is to protect you, so run and hide. if we "lose" you in the confusion, it's not our fault, but the rogues." I take the hint instantly, knowing what my friend is implying. I hug Alex tight, tears stinging my eyes. I can see that he has been waiting for an opportunity like this to help me, and I'm grateful I extended an olive branch of friendship to this wolf over a week ago.

"Thank you," I whisper, feeling his arms wrap around my waist.

"Don't worry, just protect your pup." I pull away, shocked as he taps my nose, a bemused smile on this wolf's face.

"I smelled the chemicals from the test. I'll get rid of it for you later. Just stay safe. Also, your cousin asked me to send this to you. I slipped my number in there. You can call me when you find somewhere safe, and I will find you, Laina. You're like a little sister to me now, and I've been waiting to find a reason to leave." He hands me a letter, and I nod, speechless at how much help he is giving me. He hands me a jacket and pushes me out the back door before he runs out the front. I take the opportunity to run, putting my jacket on and grabbing the bag I had stashed outside the back fence and keep running. The sounds of wolves fighting fill the forest, but I did not chance to look back. I can't look back, or else I would be captured and taken back to the cottage to resume my life as a Breeder. Being pregnant means I will not face punishment, but the security would be doubled around the cottage.

The soles of my shoes slap against the forest floor, and I clumsily make my way through the underbrush. The sounds of fighting drown out the sounds of my escape. Multiple times, I find myself changing directions to avoid the clash of wolves who fight tooth and claw to the death, with clumps of fur littering the ground. The closer to the edge of the territory, the quieter the forest becomes. With the sounds of fighting far behind me now, I make it to the edge of my pack's territory in an hour and stop before crossing it. Now, while everyone is busy with the rogues, I take the time to catch my breath. The forest is quiet away from the rogue attack, giving me peace of mind I haven't had in a long while. Remembering the letter Alex gave me, I take out the envelope I stashed into my jacket pocket, carefully putting away Alex's number before reading through the contents of the letter.

Lainy,
I hope you would read this before you got pregnant, and if you are, then I hope that it's the first set of pups you have.
Head to the treehouse we used to play in as children and grab your pink duffle bag. I know that your mind wasn't in the right place the day you were made a Breeder, but now I want you to do one thing, RUN.
Keep running until you find a mate because he or she will save you from being a Breeder.
This is the law the great Elders set out.

Stay safe, and know that we love you.
Chris and Jack

Tears flow down my face again while I read and re-read the letter. It still smells like Chris. His neat handwriting fills the paper. I knew that I had about an hour run in human form towards the treehouse, but luckily it is close to the pack border. This information makes this whole running away thing a hell of a lot easier. With a smile, I take a risk and strip my clothes off, stashing them into the duffle bag I carry now before shifting into my wolf form. Gingerly, I pick up the straps of the bag with my muzzle before dashing through the forest. I knew shifting is taboo for pregnant werewolves, but now it is a desperate situation. I need speed to make my escape, and my human form is not as fast as my wolf form.

The old oak tree comes into view after about forty minutes of running. I let out a sigh of relief, dropping my bag and shifting back to human form, then quickly re-dressing. I make my way to the ancient oak tree, the ladder to the treehouse greeting me. The scent of wolves lingers in the area, and I couldn't help but smile at the thought of pups still playing here. Looking around the base of the tree, I search for the little hollow

I used to hide in, spying my all-too-familiar pink duffle bag ready and waiting for me. I know that Chris and Jack would stock the bag with things I would need, so I decide not to bother with checking the contents. Right now, I need to leave; when I find somewhere safe, I can look inside the pink duffle bag.

The border is just a few feet away from me, waiting to accept me into the unknown and escape this cruel fate given to me. If I renounce my status as a member of Pine Paw, I will become a rogue, and so will the pup inside me. I know what I have to do. Slowly I walk towards the border, my toes just on the line as I feel the power rushing through my sneakers.

"I, Laina Starcrest, renounce my membership of this pack and henceforth become a rogue until I find my mate or a new pack to call my own." I take a step over the border and feel the snap as the connection to the pack breaks. Since my pup is only just conceived, it would have no ties to any pack until I join one. I smile and continue to run, moving wherever is farthest from my old life. I would miss my cousin and his mate, as well as Alex, Matthew, and Milly, but I need to do what is right for me and for the little one inside me. I need to find a place where there is no Breeder status and be free once again.

CHAPTER 7

Four Months Later...

The sounds of their howls were closer than the last time. I was slower than when I first escaped Pine Paw with my now-protruding stomach filled with them, the twins. But for their sake, I will keep going. I have to keep going. Currently, I'm in no man's territory where rogues like me bounce from town to town, trying to find a place where we belong. It's a region where rogues are supposed to be safe, but my pursuers tell me otherwise. The sounds of town life reach my sensitive ears from the safety of the forest trees, and I try my best to run faster. Just a few more kilometres, and I will be safe from my pursuers, from the wolves of Pine Paw who are just a stone's throw away from me.

I can hear the sounds of both wolves and humans now chasing me, realizing that some have shifted, probably to make it easier to try to persuade me to come back. Hell has a better chance of freezing over than me going back to Pine Paw.

"Don't hurt her. She is carrying my pup." Sam calls out to the wolves behind him. He knows I am pregnant. Most of my old pack knows; I guess Alex never had a chance to dispose of the pregnancy test. But no one understands why I would run away from Pine Paw, run away from being a Breeder. I left everything behind to protect my pups. I may be sixteen, but I know what is right and what is wrong. Being hunted and chased by these wolves is wrong. Being forced to accept my Alpha's seed and produce his heir is wrong. Becoming a Breeder is wrong. Everything Pine Paw did leading up to this moment is wrong. It is because of all these wrongs that I ran and will keep on running.

The safe-haven I call the town line finally comes into view, bringing renewed hope into my being. I take the chance to pick up speed and rush into the safety net. I feel some resistance at first as if some invisible force is trying to keep me out, but I keep pushing forward, and soon I am safely across, relief causing my nerves to settle down. I turn around to face my pursuers with a smug grin, slowly walking backwards as I take in each of their faces.

"You will never have this pup, and I will never be a part of your pack again," I growl out at Sam, wrapping my arms around my stomach protectively as I continue to walk backwards. So far, he only knows about one pup, and I would be damned if I let him learn that I am carrying twins.

"Look, Laina, we can talk. Just come back to the pack." Sam pleads, his body nervous as he keeps looking around. Something is off about him, but then again, I have a feeling that Sam isn't playing with a full deck of cards in his mind and that he hasn't had a right and stable mind for a while.

"How about no." I smile triumphantly and turn on my heels, walking down the road towards the town. I could hear Sam and his warriors calling out to me. They were begging me to return to them and stop walking to town—I ignored them all. I knew they just wanted me back because of the pups inside me, believing I am only carrying one. I am in no mood for their tricks and mind games. Instead, I want a poutine.

I travel along the side of the road, coming up on the sidewalk when I find one, and take in the forest surrounding the roads. It is a pleasant walk, and not having to worry about being pursued for the time being makes it easier to enjoy the fall-coloured forest. I enter the small town with my two duffle bags and keep an eye out for anywhere that might sell poutine. Many of the places were commercial restaurants like McDonald's and Tim Horton's, but neither could give me the satisfaction I needed. Then I see it and begin grinning like a Cheshire cat when the colours of a red and white checkerboard sign of a vintage-looking diner appear like some form of Messiah. I walk into the small place with lighter steps and sit at a booth, placing my bags beside me and taking out my worn-out leather wallet and placing it beside me on the table

"Long day?" I jump when a waitress quietly comes up on the other side, her face sympathetic as she takes in my tired appearance and worn-down bags. I take in her pristine white apron, her brunette hair pulled into a large bun on top of her head and a short, long-sleeved checkerboard dress that compliments her figure perfectly with her red high heels.

"Very, being pregnant is hard work." This gets the girl laughing, and I couldn't help but smile. It felt nice talking to someone not trying to capture you.

"I have three of my own, so I know the feeling. Do you know what you're having?" The waitress's friendliness brings whatever frazzled nerves I have remained down to a calmness I've missed. Being on the run for four months of my pregnancy took its toll on me.

"Twins, that's all I can tell you." The waitress nods and flips open her book, taking the pencil from behind her ear.

"So what do you want, darling?"

"Poutine with extra cheese, a vanilla milkshake, and plain cheesecake, please." She smiles at my order.

"That's what I got all the time when I was pregnant with my kids. It'll be ready in a few." With that, she leaves to ring in my order, and I heave another sigh—something I have found myself doing since running away—relaxing in the booth. From what I can tell from my walk into town, this small town is quiet, and it looks like my old pack can't come here. It is a paradise in a world of darkness that sends a light of hope just made for me.

"What do you think of living here?" I ask my protruding stomach, rubbing it gently and smiling when I feel some movements.

"Yeah, I like the idea too." I laugh. The idea that I have found a place I can call home and raise my babies in has my eyes watering with tears of joy. Pack or no pack, I will make it on my own and raise these babies, and if being in this town means I can do so here, then so be it. I felt safe the moment I crossed the town line, and this feeling of being safe is what I need in my life.

"Talking to yourself?" The same waitress returns and sets my milkshake down in front of me with a friendly smile. I couldn't help but reach for the creamy goodness and inhale it, quenching my thirst.

"I figured you were thirsty, so I brought two for you." She sets a second glass down, and I smile gratefully at her.

"Thank you," I say, reaching for the glass and setting my empty one aside.

"No problem, darling. Now-" She stops mid-sentence to sit down across from me, folding her hands on the table and looking me right in my eyes, her posture showing how serious she is.

"What is a rogue doing here on my pack's territory?" I freeze with her words, fear taking hold, and sniff the air, smelling her carefully. My eyes widen when I finally take in her scent and learn that she, too, is a werewolf.

"It's not what you think. I was running away from my old pack." I state, and she just stares at me with squinted eyes, not believing a word I say. But as a rogue, I know that trying to convince anyone of my innocence will be difficult.

"Your pack probably has Breeders like mine, and I was forced to be one, so I ran." I continue my explanation, hoping to gain her sympathy and help to settle down. I am tired of running and need a place to safely raise my pups.

"Breeders are illegal now. The Great Elders told all Alphas

this new law two years ago." The waitress nearly shouts, and I'm happy that there was only one other person here in the dining area, and he had disappeared to what I assume is the washroom a little while ago.

"B-but that's impossible. The pack I'm running from always had twenty at a time." I exclaim, my brows furrowed in confusion. *If Breeders are illegal now, then why did Sam continue it?*

"Listen, I am calling my Alpha. Then we are going to get the Elders, and we are setting that pack straight. Don't worry about paying for your food. It's on the house. You have been through a lot already, and you need a break. If you need anything, go to the counter and ask for Eeva, that's me, and I will come see what I can do." Eeva offers me a smile as her once suspicious eyes turn to ones filled with sympathy and sadness for me. Her hand reaches out for mine and squeezes it in a reassuring way filling me with all the hope I had lost over four months ago.

"O-okay." I stutter slightly as Eeva stands and leaves me alone to my thoughts. She disappears to what I assume is an office, hopefully calling her Alpha. I put my wallet away and sip at the milkshake, sighing slightly. *What had happened to me was illegal, and yet it still happened.* The thought that I was forced to be bred like an animal for someone's own gain causes a shudder to travel down my spine. I spent several days in a drug-induced state for something that was abolished two years ago. Another waitress takes me away from my swirling thoughts, placing my meal on the table. I thank her before I dig in, savouring the warmth of the poutine. I was almost done when the door to the diner opens and the bell above chimes at the arrival of a newcomer. The scent of an unfamiliar male floods the diner, causing slight tingles to run down my spine.

"Alpha Tate, this way." Eeva's voice rings clear through the diner, and my eyes widen. The reason why Sam had been terrified earlier stands just inside the door to the diner, and dread settles inside me once more for the umpteenth times this month. I am in Bloodsvain territory, and he was the Blood Alpha, the man who slaughters packs that anger him, who is possessive over the she-wolves he dates. He is mateless and feared by everyone. The Alpha of this pack is Tate Randall-Silvermoon.

I feel the power radiating off of the Alpha, feeling it get closer and envelop me as Eeva and Tate near my booth. Shivers continue to run down my spine, some are shivers of fear, but the rest are a strange feeling that I couldn't put my finger on. The Alpha's scent wraps around me, causing my body to unconsciously relax even though part of me wants to run away and move on to a new town.

"Alpha, this is the girl I told you about on the phone earlier." Slowly, I stand and turn to face her Alpha, my head bowed in submission. I am on his territory and need to show that I am not a threat if I want him to help me.

"You don't have to be afraid." His voice is gentle, something I did not expect from the infamous Blood Alpha, whose hands have been covered in blood on multiple occasions. So is his touch, as his fingers lightly touch under my chin while he raises my head, causing me to look him in the eye. My eyes widen in shock as sparks of electricity trail from his fingertips, down from where his skin touches mine and right to my toes. My breath is caught in my throat when I see his dark green coloured orbs staring back into my own, and a trace of possessiveness flickers through his gaze.

"Mate." He growls out, pulling me closer to his body, barely giving me time to press my hands against his chest to leave some room for my protruding baby bump.

"Tate, be careful. She is pregnant." Eeva warns, only to get a possessive growl from the Alpha who holds me like some delicate porcelain. I feel his arms release me for a moment, only to watch as Tate moves my bags to the other side of the booth and sits down, pulling me down carefully beside him and wrapping a protective arm around my shoulders.

"Don't be so possessive," I state boldly, glaring at the wolf before me and hating how, within our first meeting, he stakes his claim on me as if we were a bunch of barbaric beings.

"I can, and I will. You are mine." He retorts back with a bemused expression on his face as if what he says is the right answer.

"I belong to no one." We both glare at each other for a moment, neither of us wanting to back down, as the idea of him staking his claim on me rubs me the wrong way. Not realizing that Eeva had disappeared until she returns to the booth, she breaks us out of our staring contest with more milkshakes and a tray full of pastries and cookies that she slams onto the table to gather our attention.

"Look here, this girl is pregnant and already had a rough day. Now baby bro, let her be for now." Tate growls at her words, and she growls back just as threateningly. The power of two Alphas cascade over me, but I smile as I grab another vanilla milkshake and a chocolate tart. Tate's arms loosened from around me while Eeva distracts his attention away from me. The two stare at each other for a moment, linking each other, while I continue to eat the treats before me. I guess Eeva won whatever silent argument they were having as she sends a smile my way and takes my hands in her own, giving me a concerned smile.

"Now, sweetheart, what's your name?" She asks. I could feel Tate's eyes on me, waiting patiently to learn his mate's name. I guess if I wanted help, especially from these two wolves, I would have to speak.

"My name is Laina Starcrest. I came from Pine Paw pack under-"

"Samuel Lightran's rule." I nod as Tate finishes my sentence, hearing him growl loudly. Something inside me tells that Sam and Tate have a history that most likely ended badly.

"He knew about the new law and didn't stop Breeders. Tell

me whose pups you are carrying." I stay silent and look down at my hands, tears forming in my eyes. They asked me where I was from, and I answered—I did not expect some Alpha with a high and mighty attitude to start demanding things from me. I feel shame bubbling inside me. I had wanted to give my first everything to my mate, from my first kiss to my first time. Now would Tate stay with me knowing that I was forced to be a Breeder and pregnant with another wolf's pups?

"I said tell me!" He bangs his fists on the table in anger, and I flinch, the tears now falling down my face. I couldn't bring myself to tell him, but I knew deep down I had to. Tate deserves to know the truth.

"Tate, you're scaring her. I thought you said she is your mate." Eeva scolds the angry Alpha beside me, and I sense her move from across the table where she sat to my side and pull me into a hug. My body shakes as sobs wreak havoc through me, and the protective feeling that comes from the she-wolf beside me gives me the courage to speak.

"They're his. He forced himself on me to have heirs." I whisper through the sobs, feeling both of them stiffen. I knew this information must be shocking even for a normal wolf, as a rule to the Breeder is that the Alpha is forbidden to take part in producing pups. Soon, I spill the details of four months ago and what the Doctor and Sam did to me. I find myself situated in Tate's lap unbeknownst to me when I had been moved, my hands clutching his shirt as I slowly take in his scent that seems to calm my nerves.

"I'm going to-" He begins saying through clenched teeth, his hands tightening their hold around my pregnant body.

"Take Laina to your house and get her settled and cleaned up. Then, we can contact the Council and deal with this situation the right way. You know you can't slaughter the pack until they give you the go-ahead." Eeva cuts her brother off, giving him a warning glare that I catch from the corner of my tear-filled eyes.

This time, I stiffen and pull away from Tate to look him in the eye, fearing taking hold for those I care about being at the hands of his mercy.

"Not everyone is bad. Some of the Warriors refused to take part in it, and others helped me escape, like my cousin and his mate and the one Warrior who guarded me, his half-brother and sister-in-law. You can't kill them all." Even I could tell I am begging with my desperate attempt to protect those I care about. But I had to beg. I couldn't let the innocent die because of my escape. Tate relaxes against me, pulling my head to rest on his shoulder and playing with my hair.

"Make a list of those who were good to you and the other Breeders who you know of, and they can join the pack in the end. Wolves with families will be left alone. The Warriors who love partaking in the breeding will die, and so will Samuel. That's a promise, Laina." I feel his arms tighten around me. For once in a long, long time, I felt safe. I felt protected. The very thought of letting this male protect me, the wolf who seems to have more mood swings than I, a pregnant woman, have in a day, seems to be something I can consider.

"Now, let's get you home and relaxed. You need a good rest with what you've been through." He adds, pulling away and smiling at me with the most amazing smile ever. I couldn't help but be engrossed by Tate while I nod agreeing with him.

"Okay." I smile back shyly, hearing him chuckle at my reaction, letting me slide out of the booth. He takes my bags in one hand and leads me out of the diner, with his other hand protectively at the small of my back. Maybe being his mate isn't such a bad thing after all.

"Wait, take these." Once again, I hadn't noticed Eeva slip away, but she held out a bag with small boxes inside, and I could smell the delicious treats. Eeva truly is an angel sent to help me in my time of need.

"Tomorrow, we can go shopping if you want." She adds.

For once, I was happy to have come here.

"Can it wait until I get her settled in?" Tate asks, his eyes darting between his sister and me. I see a tinge of jealousy in his voice and try my best to stifle my laughter but fail as giggles erupt from my mouth.

"Sure, get some rest, Laina." I hug Eeva, my new friend, and follow Tate out the door towards a black Jeep. I climb into the passenger side and let Tate drive me to wherever "home" is. The prospect of belonging to a pack once again fills me with a sense of security I lost in Pine Paw.

CHAPTER 8

The drive is longer than I expected. We slowly leave the small town behind, and I can't help but smile contentedly as the buildings give way to the beautiful forest. The leaves are changing to the lovely colours of red, oranges, and yellows you would find in fall. Inside the Jeep, Tate turns on the seat warmer for the passenger seat, and the warmth underneath me causes my eyelids to feel heavy as I drowsily continue to watch the scenery fly past me.

I must have dozed off from the peacefulness of the drive with my newly discovered mate beside me because I soon found myself being lifted into strong arms that brought a sense of warmth and security over me, all while in a groggy stupor. Groaning, I turned my head into whoever held me, hiding my eyes from the light above and clutching at a soft fabric.

"Shh, Laina, go back to sleep, little one." A deep gentle voice whispers in my ear. I oblige, letting the darkness of a comfortable, dreamless sleep take over once more.

...

I find myself waking in an unfamiliar room, with the sweet, tantalizing scent of who I assume is my mate lingering in the air, along with the scent of freshly cooked bacon. Late morning light tries its best to filter through the soft, blue curtains, giving some light to the otherwise dark room. My eyes scan the room, finding three doors. One appears to be a closet, the second the exit into the hallway, and the third I assume is a bathroom. Pushing back the thick comforter that covers my body, I take my time to carefully sit up, resting my hand on my pregnant stomach and try my best to scan this new room.

I notice my bags right away and scramble to my feet in a panic, going through every pocket, finding the bags completely empty. Searching the room, I open the door to a walk-in closet, finding the minimal clothing I own, cleaned and hanging nicely on one side. Exiting the closet, I notice a vanity sitting just beside the large window with a brand new Kate Spade purse sitting on top with a piece of paper attached to it. Standing in front of the vanity, my hands reach for the paper. My eyes scan the note left by Tate.

Laina,
Sorry for intruding on your things, but you were in a deep sleep. I hope you like this new purse. I thought it would suit you.

Tate

I sigh with relief and a bit of giddiness as I look inside the purse, noticing my wallet and booklet of numbers inside. Tate has a notorious name in the werewolf community as a ruthless wolf who demolishes and massacres packs that anger the Blood Alpha. But... this big bad Alpha wolf seems to be a softy when it comes to me. Putting the note away in my purse, I continue to explore the room.

I smile triumphantly when I find a large bathroom with a clawfoot bathtub to soak in. After relieving my full bladder that the twins press against, I search the bathroom for some bubble bath. I find a vanilla-scented bubble bath and start the bath, using half the bottle of the scented liquid. Foamy bubbles soon cover the surface of the bath water. The thought of a long soak in a bubble bath brought tears to my eyes. It has been a while since I last enjoyed a bubble bath, and when running for both your life and the children inside you, it is hard to find a place to enjoy even a shower.

I carefully undress and climb into the clawfoot tub, the scent of vanilla wrapping around me. The heat of the water is comforting, and my sore muscles begin to relax. The twins must have agreed with me as they gently move inside me, causing a soft smile to spread on my face.

"What do you think of this, Alpha?" I ask my stomach, gently rubbing the baby bump. I giggle when they kick at my hands harder than earlier, taking their movements as a positive response. Maybe being here is turning into a good thing. The quiet bathroom fills with steam and the scent of vanilla, causing my still-tired body to become slightly drowsy again. I decide that now would be a good time to scrub my body clean and rinse off the suds with the shower hose before I doze off into dreamland and accidentally drown in the water. Once fully cleaned and the sore muscles from being on the run relaxed, I climb out of the now empty tub and wrap a large, fluffy, black towel around my body. Part of me did not want to leave the warm room, but my stomach is starting to protest its need for food. After towel-drying my hair, I exit the bathroom and head into the walk-in closet to pick out a pair of leggings and a baggy long-sleeved shirt. I couldn't help but sigh, knowing that the shirt I',m wearing is a little too snug, but there is nothing I can do until I go shopping for proper clothing to fit my growing body.

Exiting the closet, a knock on the door catches my attention, causing me to turn towards it with suspicion. Taking a deep breath to steady my nervous heart, I reach for the nearest object I can do damage with—a lamp—and position myself just to the side in a defensive stance, ready to attack whoever is on the other side of the wooden door.

"Come in," I call out, watching the door open to reveal Tate.

"Good mor- Wait, were you going to hit me with that?" I sigh with relief and put the lamp back, facing my mate, who gives me a puzzled look.

"No, I was going to hit whoever I didn't know with it." I correct, getting a chuckle from him that sends my heart fluttering.

"I thought you would like to know that food is ready, and I brought you a shirt since yours looked too small when I was cleaning your clothes." I smile at Tate's considerate thought, thanking him while I take the offered shirt. Slipping out of the tight long-sleeved shirt, I pull on the soft, cotton, black long-sleeved V-neck shirt that smells faintly like him. Now feeling much more comfortable, I stretch, loving the fact I can move freely once again.

"Not shy around guys?" It wasn't a question, but how Tate words his statement causes me to blush slightly in embarrassment.

"Sorry. I am used to changing in front of my cousin and his mate because they're gay and everything. You should have seen their faces when they brought me back new clothes and have a fashion show in our living room." I apologize, giving Tate an explanation at my comfort around men I put my trust in. I squeak in surprise when strong arms pull me towards a chiselled chest, Tate's scent enveloping my senses.

"Don't apologize to me. You are my mate. You should be comfortable around me." He says, kissing the top of my head. I couldn't help but snuggle into him, the sense of security returning. If this is how a mate is supposed to be, then count me sucked in and give me a contract to sign.

"Now, come on. Let's go eat." He lets go of me, and I instantly miss his warmth. I smile happily when he takes my hand and leads me out of the room. The hallway is a light grey colour, with pictures of Tate, Eeva, and three young boys placed every now and then. Being led down the dark wooden stairs, I try my best to take a peek around the front entrance and the next hallway until I stand in a large, bright kitchen. I couldn't help but smile at the thought of baking inside here while I look at the large counter with a high-end stove and a door to what I assume is the pantry. The thought of the recipes I love so much, filling the house with their delicious scent and children running around, is feeling close to becoming a reality.

"Sit over there, and I'll bring you some food. I know you've had a rough time, so I want you to get some rest and take it easy for now." Tate directs me to a breakfast nook in the corner of the kitchen, situated under large windows on either side. I smile at how pampering he sounds. The image of a cruel Alpha I once imagined him to be is slowly dissolving into this sweet mate image he displays now. I sit down and take the time to fully look at my mate. He has dark chestnut-coloured hair, similar to my own, with lighter natural highlights thrown about. His hair is cut short and styled messily; my fingers itch to run through his hair and feel just how soft his locks are. His broad shoulders connect to solid muscular arms, the same arms that have held me multiple times since meeting yesterday. One thing is for sure, Tate is fit and lean, his body radiating power as an Alpha's body should. His dark green eyes reminded me of the forest in the summer. His eyes are warm and welcoming. I know that if I stare too deeply into these eyes of his, then I will lose myself to him.

"Here you go. Over easy eggs, bacon and hash browns." Tate's voice breaks me from my thoughts as he places a full plate in front of me. My stomach is grumbling from the wonderful aroma.

"And some blueberry vanilla tea." He adds, chuckling at my reaction to the food.

"Thank you." I smile graciously at my mate, taking a sip of the herbal tea before digging into my eggs. Tate soon joins me with a plate of his own and adds two pieces of toast to my plate, which I use to soak up the warm egg yolks. The distinctive smell of coffee hits my nose from the green mug Tate sips from, his eyes looking everywhere but at me as my nose scrunches up at the strong scent. We sit there in silence for a moment before he sighs and looks at my stomach. I see the reluctance to accept my pregnancy reflected in the depth of his eyes.

"You really did not know about it being illegal, about Breeders being illegal?" He asks with concern etched into his face. I couldn't help but put my left hand on my stomach, nodding yes to answer his question, receiving another deep sigh from Tate.

"I guess only a few knew about the new rule. The Beta pair probably knew. Most wolves probably just decided to ignore it to get free sex." I reply quietly as I think about Abby and her attitude. It all makes sense with how her behaviour took a one-eighty.

"They are a bunch of morons if you ask me," Tate growls out in frustration, rubbing his hand against his face.

"Not all of them." I look up to see him staring at me, his eyes filled with love and jealousy. I start to have doubts and wonder if Tate would protect my pups as his own or if I would have to leave this wolf behind. The thought of the latter causes pain to rip through my heart.

"I will protect you, but I don't like the fact that the pups you are carrying aren't mine." I sigh at his angry words, looking down at my empty plate. I get he must feel terrible knowing that the mate he has waited for is pregnant for someone else, but it's not like he waited for me. Everyone knew of the many girls he had dated before becoming an Alpha. I used to feel sorry for the wolf who ends up as his mate, but seeing how concerned and gentle he is with me makes me happy in a weird way.

"Look, Tate, I am not in the mood for arguing. We just met. I want to get to know you and for you to get to know me, but whether you like it or not, I am keeping these babies." I state clearly and carefully, standing up to put my dishes in the sink. I could feel his eyes on me as I make my way out of the kitchen and into the next room that turns out to be the living room. My eyes instantly go to the house phone located just on the desk by the large bay window, and I walk over to pick it up. Scanning through the contacts, I find the person I am looking for—Eeva—and press the call button.

"I told you to let her sleep, you idiot. She's pregnant, for Goddess' sake." She answers, more like yells, into the phone before I could say anything.

"Um A) Ouch my ear-" I shout, switching the phone to my left ear while I massage the abused right ear.

"And B) Want to go shopping? I need clothes for my ever-expanding baby bump." I continue, offering an olive branch to the wolf that will be my sister-in-law.

"Sorry about that, Laina. I thought you were Tate calling. The idiot has called me about ten times wanting to wake you up since you've slept like the dead for a day. And yes, I would love to go shopping. I'll be there in a few." She hangs up, and I giggle at the phone before putting it back in its receiver. I make my way back up the stairs, return to the room I woke up in, and quickly grab my new purse. After washing my face and brushing my teeth, I head back down the stairs only to see Tate standing in the front hallway with a suspicious look on his handsome face.

"Where are you going?" He asks, his eyes looking at the purse in my hand while I look for a pair of shoes in the hallway closet.

"I'm going shopping with your sister," I reply, slipping my worn-out sneakers onto my feet and looking inside my purse to double-check that I have everything.

"I am your mate. I should go with you." He growls possessively, his arms landing on either side of my head against the wall I am leaning on. I could see his emotions swirling in the depth of his eyes as I wonder what his problem is. I get we are mates, but I needed this, some sense of normalcy again. Going out with a she-wolf brings this normalcy back.

"And I am a free person who can go anywhere I want,

and I will not be treated any differently. I became a slave to my old pack before running away; I will not be treated as one in my new pack!" I retort, raising my voice but keeping the volume lower than a yell. Shock fills Tate's eyes, replacing all of the other thoughts, as he stares at me in disbelief. A blush covers my cheeks when I realize what I have said, turning to look away for a moment.

"Wait? Your new pack?" He questions, his fingers tilting my head to look back at him.

"I figured since we are mates, I should join. If you don't want m-" My words are cut off as Tate's lips are pressed to mine. The kiss is sweet and gentle. I could feel his possessiveness and care he pours into this single kiss as his hands move to wrap me in an embrace.

"I want you." He says when he pulls away, kissing my forehead. I couldn't help the grin that spreads across my face as he tucks my head under his chin, hugging me to him.

"Just get yourself a cell phone so that I can reach you and so you can call me." He adds with a sigh. I knew I won my time to go out with Eeva and get away for a bit with these words. The front door swings open, and Eeva sticks her head in, looking around as if afraid of being caught.

"Sorry, I was waiting for the yelling to stop before I came in." Eeva states, and I laugh at her.

"So, my mate has the punks for a few hours; you have a meeting to go to Tate and don't worry, Laina is in good hands." My new friend states and pulls me from her brother's arms and leads me to the front door.

"Bye, bro, love you." She says in a singsong voice, pushing me out the door and out of his reach as I laugh at her antics.

"Go, go, go! He is possessive and did not like the way I took you away from him." She says as if she is a soldier ordering me about as I climb into her Hummer. She speeds out of the drive-way just in time for a pissed-off Tate to run out after us, his eyes glaring at his sister as he shakes his head.

"To the mall!" She exclaims, and I sit back, clutching at my stomach that is slightly sore from laughing so hard.

"Hey, if you pass a Tim Horton's, can we stop so I can get a white hot chocolate?" I ask

"Sure, one thing about our lovely Canada is that Tim Horton's are everywhere." She answers, and I laugh again. I had a feeling that Eeva and I will be very close, almost like true sisters.

CHAPTER 9

"I don't need all these clothes!" I exclaim in frustration as I exit the changing room, only to spot Eeva throwing more clothes into the shopping cart. I can't help but shake my head at the brunette woman as she picks clothes for me from dresses to pants, casual to formal. I had a feeling if I let her continue, she would turn whatever savings I have into nothing.

"One, you do. I even threw in clothes you can use for after you deliver your babies. Two, they're cute and will fit any occasion, and as the future Luna, you need them. And three, they fit you." I couldn't argue with Eeva's logic. All the clothes she has chosen for me are in a style I like, and many were close to the pre-pregnancy size that I can fit into once the twins are born. With a sigh, I follow behind Eeva as she pushes the cart towards the counter, her eyes scanning around if she missed any other article of clothing from this store that would suit me. I had a feeling she did not get out to shop much and is using me to enjoy the opportunity to shop until we drop. At this point, I am ready to drop.

"Come on, preggers, as much as I would love to stay here at the mall, we, unfortunately, don't have all day. You need to look good to see the Elders." I stop at her words, shocked. Not many people can get an appointment right away and would have to wait months just to get anything changed from the leaders of the werewolves. The Elders—ancient werewolves from the first packs—are the ones who make the laws that we have to follow; even the Alpha King who rules over wolf kind needs to listen to these Elders to some degree. They approve of new packs and decide whether war between two packs would be a good or bad decision. They mainly focus on keeping the peace between the packs and presiding over the annual National meeting each spring.

"You managed to get their approval for an audience?" I ask in disbelief. Having Breeders at Pine Paw must have been a huge taboo for the Elders to push my case to the top of their list.

"Yes, I managed to get an appointment. It's easy considering Bloodsvain is one of the oldest packs in Canada." Eeva answers, her head held high with pride. I can't help but wrap my arms around her in a tight hug as best as I can. It dawned on me that running into Bloodsvain territory is the best thing I have ever done since being declared a Breeder.

"Okay, girly, enough sappiness. Let's go check out and head to the next store." She chuckles, hugging me back. I pull away from my new friend, her eyes slightly teary with concern for my well-being and the situation I had been forced into. We continue towards the counter. The store clerk takes each item Eeva places in front of her and scans them. I decide not to look at the total price, knowing that I will probably stress about how much money I would have to spend and proceed to fish my debit card out from my wallet.

"Should I put everything on the usual tab, Miss Eeva?" The Clerk asks as she continues to carefully fold and bag the clothing.

"Yes, please, Anne, that would be great. By the way, this is my sister-in-law, Laina." Eeva replies back, taking the many bags of clothing before ushering me out of the store.

"I could have paid!" I state, slightly pouting at the feeling of being treated as a child. I preferred doing things for myself, something I had gotten used to with my parent's passing.

"I know, sweetie, but you are going to be a member of our pack and the Luna. You should get used to being treated like one of us. Besides, our pack owns the town that everything is located on as well as many other businesses in Canada. If you think spending money on you is going to cause Bloodsvain to go bankrupt, think again." Eeva explains with a smile on her face. I guess being Tate's mate did bring benefits, but I still felt a little uneasy.

"But Eeva –" I begin to protest.

"No buts, Laina. As my sister-in-law and Luna, you will allow yourself to be pampered." Eeva cuts me off, her voice stern like my mother's used to be when I was being unreasonable. I sigh in defeat, deciding to agree with Eeva's reasoning. I will be the Luna of Bloodsvain soon, so I had to just accept everything that came with it, including being allowed to spend Tate's money.

"Fine, but let's drop the bags off at the car before we continue shopping, okay?" I relent, seeing a wide smile spread across my friend's face.

"Sounds like a plan then." She agrees, leading me towards the parking lot where we deposit the bags from the first store into her Hummer and continue our shopping. After two more stores, I convince the energetic she-wolf to stop at the Chinese buffet for a late lunch. Honestly, I just need a moment to sit and relax my swollen feet.

"After lunch, do you want to head home?" Eeva asks, shoving a whole chicken ball into her mouth. I open my mouth to answer when movement from inside me catches my attention, and I can't help but giggle, placing my hand on where one of the babies kicks.

"One minute, give me your hand," I whisper in awe, taking Eeva's outstretched hand and placing it on my stomach. A couple of seconds later, two sets of feet kick out at us, causing wide grins to spread across our faces. Love blooms for my babies as we sit at our table in silence, the smell of Chinese food and the soft sound of a zither playing in the background, bringing back the sense of normalcy in my life.

"Would you like to shop for them? We could start their nursery. I'm positive Tate will be happy to see you smiling." Eeva suggests in a low voice, not wanting to break this serene moment. With a small smile, I nod, my eyes still on my pregnant stomach. Now free from my Breeder status, I can raise my babies in a room they can grow up in. This thought brings tears to my eyes. I could only blame my emotional state on the pregnancy hormones coursing through my body.

"I would really like that, please, but let's keep the colours neutral for now." I agree with Eeva's suggestion. We finish our meal and leave the buffet to search for children and baby stores. I couldn't help but think back on the horrible shopping experience I had with Abby four months ago and comparing it to this one with Eeva. Eeva spent the time comparing cribs and bassinets with me. Having someone like Eeva who waited patiently while I search through every item the stores have to offer for my babies brought happiness surging inside me. I am grateful for how Eeva has treated me so far in these last two days. She is kind, patient, caring, and sort of motherly, but not once did she pity me; only sympathy and concern are ever shown in her expressive eyes. Once everything is ordered and the delivery day for the twins' nursery furniture is set, Eeva and I make a final stop at the Bell store in search of a new cellphone for me. I find a Samsung phone that I like, and we set up a new account, finally ending our shopping trip.

"Let's not 'shop till we drop' anymore." I yawn, climbing into Eeva's car and clicking the seatbelt into place. My body felt sore and exhausted, but this trip ended in success. I never realized how badly I needed something as normal as a shopping day with a girlfriend until now, as Eeva shifts the gear into drive, and we proceed to head back home. Home. That word brought a grin as large as the Cheshire cat's to my face. I had found a home to live in and watch my twins grow.

"Okay, we'll just shop till we have what we need then." My friend says sarcastically to my earlier complaint, causing me to roll my eyes at her. Knowing Eeva, if I let her drag me to another shopping spree, she would keep shopping even well after I drop with exhaustion.

"Have you decided their names yet?" Eeva asks, motioning to my stomach. I smile down, rubbing my pregnant belly.

"No, not yet. I haven't learned their genders, so I am waiting until after they are born." I answer, catching Eeva nod understandingly.

"Well, you still have a few months left, so don't worry." She reassures me, and I smile. But my smile lasts for a few seconds before I turn my head to look out of the passenger window and sigh. There was one nagging problem at the back of my mind. One I've been wondering since running away with the thoughts of finding a pack to call home or finding my mate.

"Okay, ask it, Laina," Eeva says after two songs on the radio fill the silence between us.

"Do you think Tate will get over the fact that these aren't his pups?" I finally say with worry in my voice, my eyes searching Eeva's face.

"Yes, he will. He is just pissed off that you had to go through what you did." Eeva says quietly. I couldn't tell if she is trying to reassure herself or me with these words, but a hopeful smile spreads across my face. I know that things between Tate and me will be hard with my pregnancy situation, but I hope he will eventually accept my babies. I spent four months running away to protect them, and no one, not even my mate, will take them away from me.

Eeva and I both go into our own thoughts after that. I decided to take out my new cellphone from my purse, enjoying the feel of the latest Samsung device in my hand as the large screen comes to life. Taking the notebook I had stored the numbers of important wolves in my life, I begin to slowly add everyone into my new phone—starting with Chris, Jack and Alex—and text each person, letting them know it's me and that I am safe.

As we drive out of the town and towards the forest road, I catch glimpses of wolves running through. I couldn't help but smile as they stop to bow towards us respectfully before continuing about their business. I couldn't wait to be able to shift and run with them.

"Hey, Eeva, what is your phone number?" I ask with my eyes still on the forest. A larger black wolf than the rest catches my attention, his forest green eyes turning to stare back. Something in me told me it is Tate, and I couldn't help but enjoy his majestic wolf form.

"I think it's..." She trails off, thinking for a moment before rattling off the numbers. I quickly key in her cellphone number into my contact list, saving it and sending a quick text. She pulls off the main road and into a smaller dirt road before pulling over to quickly add my new number to her contacts, a grin on her face.

"There now we have each other's number and can talk whenever," I exclaim with a grin, laughing as she widens her eyes and places a hand over her chest.

"Oh darling, you make my life complete." She fake cries in joy, causing me to go into a laughing fit with her antics.

"You know, you look younger when you laugh. I mean for a twenty-year-old who is a soon-to-be mom you-" She muses, looking at me with a grin.

"I'm not twenty." I cut her off, watching her eyes widen with shock this time.

"You're not?" Eeva asks with skepticism.

"No." Is my honest reply with a grimace on my face.

"Then how old are you, Laina?" I could tell that Eeva is

weary, her eyes showing even more sympathy than yesterday.

"As of May this year, I turned sixteen," I admitted, twirling a lock of hair with my finger. I look outside to watch the early October breeze rustle through the trees, feeling a little ashamed. Leaves fall in a twirling dance to the ground. The car is silent for a while, and I look to Eeva to see her eyes unfocused. I guess she is mind linking someone, Probably Tate. When her eyes regain focus, she starts driving once again, a frown on her face.

"You told Tate, didn't you?" I say, feeling both relieved and a little worried. *What will he do knowing my age now?*

"Yes. I'm sorry, Laina, but Tate needed to know that you are considered a minor even if pack laws dictate wolves to be adults at sixteen." Eeva replies. I could see the worry in her eyes as I turn back to look out the window and watch the scenery.

"Thank you," I whisper as we pass by a few log cabins, cottages and houses that I assume are homes to pack members.

"For what?" She asks with a smile in my direction.

"For being a true friend and treating me like an adult."

"Why wouldn't I treat you like an adult or be a friend to you? You're practically my sister now that you're my baby brother's mate." She reasons, and I smile.

"I'm glad for that too."

"Me too, Laina. Even though Tate had girlfriends, he always kept searching for his mate. My brother has anger issues, but I haven't seen him lose control in the last two days since meeting you." Eeva adds. I could hear the relief in her voice as she talks about Tate. I hated knowing that he had other girls in his life before me but felt like a hypocrite considering I am pregnant for someone else. This whole situation is just fucked up.

Eeva decides to change the radio station, and we begin to belt out the songs we know. The mood lightens as she points out the pack house—a five-story mansion that I am told was built seven hundred years ago—and other important buildings in the pack. We pass by an elementary school for children, a pack hospital, and a library built to help the younger wolves study. Finally, we arrive home, and I take in the other houses scattered about that I missed in our mad dash to escape to the mall this morning.

"My brother's house has six bedrooms. I think right now you are in one of the guestrooms, so I'll wash your new clothes and the baby clothes, then bring it to your room." Eeva says as we enter the house with the bags from our shopping trip.

"I can help," I state, following her to the laundry room that is located on the first floor of this massive place just to the side of the kitchen—thank the Goddess for first-floor laundry rooms because I hate stairs.

"Laina, how far along are you?" Eeva questions as we set the bags on the floor in the pristine room, the machines all high-end and state-of-the-art perfection for the cleanest laundry possible.

"Somewhere between four to four and a half months," I say, placing a hand on my stomach.

"Well, a she-wolf gives birth to her pups at five to six months, so no work for you. You sit and look pretty while I help get you set up." Eeva orders with her no-nonsense motherly tone.

"But Eeva!"

"No buts, go sit." She cuts me off, ushering me out of the laundry room and towards the living room.

"Okay, fine, I will. But you call me if you need help." I concede as she hugs me and disappears once again into the laundry room.

I smile and head to the kitchen to make tea, realizing that it is five-thirty in the afternoon. I figure that Tate will be hungry when he gets back from dealing with his pack, and I want to surprise my mate with dinner. Fluttering around the kitchen, I familiarize myself with where everything is placed as I gather the ingredients and equipment I would need from the fridge, cupboards and pantry.

"What you making?" Strong arms wrap around me, and soft lips find a spot on my neck as a warm body that sends happy shivers down my spine presses against me.

"Chicken and waffles," I reply, a smile on my face as I lean into Tate. His scent wraps around me as his body tenses slightly with our contact before he relaxes into me once again. I couldn't help but notice that he towers above me, my head just reaching past his shoulder, making my frame feel small and safe inside his embrace.

"Sounds delicious. Do you want any help?" He asks, his lips finding my neck once again as he plants soft, gentle kisses.

"S-sure, do you know where the waffle maker is?" I couldn't help the flustered tremor in my voice with his close proximity. With a chuckle, Tate lets me go and walks to a cupboard I have yet to go through. I miss his warm touch, the mate bond between us simmering gently in the air. Returning to my side, I begin to instruct Tate on what to do with this recipe, watching his large hands skilfully mix the waffle batter as I work on breading and shallow pan-frying the chicken.

"So, what were you learning in school before you..." Tate asks once we engross ourselves in the task of cooking. His voice trails off at the end, neither of us wanting to bring up the Breeder subject.

"I was going for interior design at the local college. I always loved creating and decorating when I was growing up. After my parents' death, I ended up shutting myself off from everyone and focused on school. It allowed me to bypass grade school and took me about two years to finish high school courses since I took courses in the summer and online. I never felt like a normal teenager since many kids my age were hanging out with friends and partying, and all I wanted was to help out my cousin and his mate. Chris took me in when he was eighteen. I felt that he had to raise me and thought I would build a career to help him out. He surprised me by enrolling me in the college courses on my fifteenth birthday. I was only two years away from getting my degree before being told my role…" I felt happy talking about my past up until recent events, as well as my dream of being an Interior Designer. I wish I could bring my sketchbook from my room in Chris' house to show Tate the work I put in, but I knew that that would probably never happen. My fingers itched for a sketchbook, some sketch pencils, and a sturdy ruler to come up with concepts and designs for the rooms in this house. I notice that it has more of a cold, distant feel to the living room, the front hallway and the entrance, and I guess that the other rooms that I have yet to explore are empty and cold and in need of re-decorating. This house definitely needs a bit of a makeover and a woman's touch.

"If you want, there is a study down the hall with a computer. It's my office, and you can use it to take courses online from your college while you redesign one of the rooms upstairs for your own office." Tate offers, his face lowered in a bashful way while a slight pink tinge colours his cheeks. My eyes widen as I process his words before I fling my arms around him, as best as I can with my pregnant belly protruding out. The rumours of Tate being a heartless monster seem to vanish with how warm and caring he is towards me. Stretching up on my toes, I pull Tate's head towards mine, kissing him quickly with a peck on the lips in my excited state.

"Thank you so much!" I say happily when we pull away, surprise and shock on his face as he holds me in his embrace.

"Anything to make you happy, Laina. I can't wait to see what you do with the house to make it more like a home. To be honest with you, I usually stay at the pack house to do work. I haven't had a reason to stay here other than to grab clean clothes until you came around." I watch as another blush creeps across his face, the butterflies fluttering around my heart at his confession. We go back to cooking our dinner as we talk about our day. I laugh when I tell Tate about all the stores I went to, and he sighs.

"I have a feeling Eeva went overboard with shopping and snuck stuff in for herself, didn't she?" He questions, and I grin mischievously. He was right, though, as Eeva had spent some time shopping for herself, but I refused to snitch on her even if Tate is her brother.

"Finally getting along?" Eeva asks as she walks into the kitchen just as Tate and I finish cooking. She helps us set the table as I stretch my tired body.

"We always get along," Tate answers, pulling me to his side and rubbing my back. I couldn't help but smile at the small massage, my tense muscles relaxing even more.

"Well, that's good to hear. Laina, I put the clothes in your room and the baby stuff in a basket for when you find a room to decorate." Eeva states, snatching a piece of fried chicken from the plate and snacking on it.

"Now, I have to go. My mate and the pups have a surprise waiting for me. Enjoy your meal, you two." With that, Eeva saunters out of the house. I could hear Tate sigh with relief, a boyish grin on his face as he helps me sit at the breakfast nook in the kitchen.

"I love my sister, but Hurricane Eeva can be too much to handle." I couldn't help but laugh at his helpless look as he walks towards the fridge and brings a jug of orange juice and two glasses to the table.

"Now, let's eat!" He exclaims, pouring each of us a glass of orange juice. It doesn't take long for the both of us to load our plates with the soft and fluffy waffles and crispy chicken. After a moment of comfortable silence and the sound of cutlery clinking across the plates, I look at Tate with a shy smile.

"Do you want to get to know each other and play a round of questions?" My question comes out quietly, almost a whisper. I could see the smile spreading on my mate's face with my initiative in getting to know him as he takes a bite of a piece of chicken dripping with real Canadian maple syrup.

"Sure, what's your favourite colour?" He questions back, a grin spreading across my face.

"It's a deep green, like your eyes. They remind me of the forest. What's your favourite food?" I answer, smiling at the thought of being able to run in the forest again.

"Believe it or not, it's actually chicken and waffles. Eeva would have it ready for me every time I enter her diner. But now I think yours is actually the best I've ever had." I could feel my face heating up with his compliment at my recipe, smiling at the memory of how I learned it.

"It's a recipe my mother taught me. I have all of her recipes memorized." I could see his eyes softening with the mention of my parents. Our game of "Questions" continues while the pile of food slowly disappears between us. Deciding to move to a more comfortable area, Tate places the dishes into the sink to be washed later, and we head to the living room. Sitting on either end of the large sofa, Tate and I start chatting about our childhood. I couldn't help but feel more drawn to him as we slowly get to know each other. Before I know it, I am comfortably curled up against him as we cuddle. The lighting in the room is soft and intimate.

"You should go to sleep." Tate whispers, his hand drawing soft circles on my back as I yawn for the eighth time in the last three minutes.

"I don't want to," I whisper back, looking up at him and staring into his eyes. He chuckles and lowers his forehead to mine, rubbing our noses together.

"Then how about we get ready for bed and you cuddle with me in my room while we watch something on T.V.? This way, if you fall asleep, you'll be comfortable." He reasons, planting a kiss on my forehead. I could feel myself growing drowsy, but I wanted to keep talking

"Okay then." I agree. I head upstairs into my room to find all the new clothes bought today put away neatly in the closet. I couldn't help but smile and send a thank-you text to Eeva before picking out a pair of baggy P.J. pants and a soft cotton T-shirt for bed. Once changed, I make my way down the dark hallway towards the room with light filtering through the door. The room is filled with Tate's scent as I look everywhere for him before climbing into his massive bed under the covers. A door opens, and out walks Tate from what I realize is the bathroom with a pair of P.J. pants slung low around his waist, and his chiselled torso bare for me to enjoy. He climbs into bed, reaching for the T.V. remote on his side of the bed, before pulling me close to his side. He flicks through the channels looking for something to watch, finally landing on Finding Nemo.

"Really?" I ask, laughing at his choice of movie.

"What? It's a classic, babe." He states with a roll of his eyes, and I giggle again.

"Okay, okay, we can watch it." I concede as I snuggle closer to Tate. I smile when his hand continues to rub circles on me, his head leaning towards my direction every now and then to kiss the top of my head. Sometime during the first few minutes of the movie, my eyelids grow heavy, and I find myself falling asleep.

CHAPTER 10

The first week of living with Tate flies by as he and I get used to the routine of living together. I had slowly moved my clothing and other items into Tate's room. The vanity I found in the guestroom I woke up in on the first day in this house has been moved to sit in front of the large bay window that faces the backyard. Tate let me explore the house as much as I wanted, where I found the basement with a large workout room on the second day. I couldn't help but squeal with glee when I saw all of the workout equipment, going as far as doing some light workout, with a worried and panicking Tate frantically trying to keep the heavier weights away from me. Spoilsport.

There were times when walking around the forest with my mate when we would pass by his pack members, and his possessive side would show. The first time I convinced him to go for a walk with me, a Warrior got too close, thinking a rogue was attacking his Alpha. I had to pull Tate's black wolf form by the scruff of his neck off of the Warrior while screaming and yelling at him. I could tell with just my touch alone he visibly relaxed. With me distracting Tate, the Warrior was able to run free to a safe distance, and Tate wrapped his huge furry body around me, his black fur warming me up as his scent rubbed into me. I introduced myself as Tate's mate, my hands scratching my mate's ear as the Warrior stared back. With a respectful bow, he left us alone to continue our walk in the forest that day. I guess that Warrior warned the rest of the wolves as a way to stop them from accidentally attacking me since we rarely saw anyone else. Even when we did see another wolf, they would stay a respectful distance away from Tate and I, greeting us with a respectful bow.

I can't help but relish the sight of the calm forest as I sit on a fallen log. Tate is running around being chased by small children in his wolf form as Eeva, and I watch on. Eeva's mate is Tate's Beta, and due to pack business, he is on a mission to make a treaty with a new smaller pack and will return later tonight. For the last few days, the four of them have joined us for meals and outings around the territory.

"How is Tate now with you being pregnant?" Eeva asks as her youngest, Jonathan, manages to jump onto Tate's back, getting a cheer from his two brothers while the pup clings to his uncle's fur. I couldn't help but chuckle at the young pups with their uncle. It makes me excited for when the twins are born, and Tate could play with them like this.

"He still has some issues with it, but he is coming around. Honestly, if you had seen him when I was designing my office, you would have thought they were his pups. He is such a worry-wart and wouldn't allow me to paint or move any furniture. Don't get me started with even doing a small workout. I'm positive the only weights I'm allowed to touch are the one- and two-pound weights." I rant, feeling annoyed by how my mate acts. Two days ago, the paint and furniture, as well as the laptop and electronics for my office, arrived. I tried my best to carry the lighter objects up the stairs, but Tate would take them from my hands and make me wait inside the room. When he stepped out to take a call, I had decided to start painting, nearly spilling the can of paint when he came in to lecture me about resting while he does all the work. It took the whole day, but I managed to get the room decorated, barely having to move a muscle and being very annoyed by Tate's attitude around me doing any form of work. But it does make me smile, knowing how caring he is towards me and my pregnant state. I know deep down that he will make a wonderful father to the twins.

"Speaking of that office of yours, how is it going for you?" Eeva asks. I had started my college courses back up again three days ago. It felt nice having something to do when left alone at home. Tate had gone out and surprised me the day my office was completed by buying all the art materials I would want plus more that I stored in the closet.

"It's going really well. I love having a space of my own. I somehow managed to get caught up with all the work I missed out on." I answer, leaning back on the tree behind me and taking a deep breath. I haven't become a member of the pack just yet, and neither have I taken on the role of Luna yet. Tate and Eeva suggest I wait until after giving birth as the ritual may cause harm to the twins. Instead, I spend my free time when not with Tate or Eeva, doing my schoolwork or learning about the pack and my duties as a Luna. Some things I do now with Bloodsvain are look over the businesses and go through the members' list to see who needs to be given a role in the pack. Tate had asked me to redesign a few of the buildings they own, and I happily took on the challenge.

"Well, that's good. Finish your school so you can start redesigning the pack house. Goddess only knows it needs an update." My friend chuckles. I feel a wet nose sniffing at my hand and turn to see Tate looking at me, a bemused expression on his wolf face.

"Is it time to head home?" I ask, my hand reaching out to scratch under his chin as the three boys slowly trudge over.

"Mom, can we play with Uncle Tate again later tomorrow?" Vinny asks. The eldest of the three has his brother Jonathan sleeping on his back as the second pup comes up behind him. I couldn't help but give Andy a hug as he sleepily rubs his eyes. I hear the sound of Tate shifting into his human form and putting on clothes before picking up the pup, taking him from my arms, and wrapping an arm around my shoulders.

"They are all tuckered out and need their bed now. Let's get Eeva and the boys home, then we can have a quiet night." Tate says as Andy falls asleep against his uncle's shoulder. The sight of Tate holding a pup causes me to smile. I couldn't wait for the next few weeks to fly by so we could raise the twins. Eeva takes Jonathan from Vinny as the six of us walk through the forest towards Eeva's house. I sigh when my body sinks into the rocking chair on her front porch. My mate brings his nephews up to their rooms.

I watch the leaves on the oak tree fall to the ground. Fall is my favourite time of year, with beautiful colours and the chance to wear cozy warm sweaters. The nice weather allows me to run in my wolf form without dying from the heat of the glaring sun or my thick fur in the summer. I especially love being able to dress up for Halloween, the only time I am very childish.

"Comfortable?" I look up to see Tate smiling down at me from his spot as he leans against the door frame. I smile at my mate and hold my hand out for him, watching him take it and lean forward to leave a kiss on the back of my hand.

"Can we get a rocking chair for our porch?" I ask as Tate helps me to my feet and holds me close in a gentle hug.

"Sure. We can get two if you want, one for each of us?" He suggests, causing me to grin. The idea of having a comfortable rocking chair on the porch makes me sigh contentedly. We say our farewells to Eeva before getting into Tate's Jeep and driving home. Tate decides to order us a pizza for dinner, and we curl up on the couch watching *Say Yes to the Dress*. Tate won't admit it, but I got him into the show. Yesterday, I caught him secretly watching it in his study, so I took a quick video to send to Eeva. Apparently, she couldn't stop laughing when she saw the serious look on Tate's face as he commented that some girl should have chosen the Lazaro dress.

"Have you decided on baby names yet, Laina?" Tate asks as I take a large bite of the meat lover's pizza.

"Not yet. I have a few names in mind right now, but we can decide when they are born." I answer, smiling sheepishly at

Tate. I watch his reaction closely, catching a slight smile playing on his lips.

"Yeah, we can decide when they are born." He agrees, leaning over to kiss my cheek. I felt happiness burst inside at Tate's reply. I could feel the shift in his feelings on the babies inside me, and it is shifting for the good.

After a long day, we decide to head to bed early. I loved the feeling of falling asleep in his arms as his scent wraps around me. Soon, we will be able to complete the mating ritual. I just have to wait another three months for when the babies are born for us to be together forever.

CHAPTER 11

Pain!

Pain is all I can feel, gripping my body with terror, as I wake up, clutching at my sides. I let out a scream as a spasm rocks through my body, causing me to curl up as best as I can. Something inside me tells me that something is wrong. Tears are streaming down my face.

"Tate!" I scream out, praying that the sleeping wolf beside me wakes up quickly. I don't know how much of this pain I can endure. Feeling my mate jump out of bed, I catch his green orbs glowing, searching for danger. His bright eyes soon land on my curled-up form. I whimper as another wave of pain shoots through me, the tears continuing to flow.

"What's wrong, baby?" I see the panic-stricken look on Tate's face as he rushes around the bed and to my side, his hands brushing away the hair that sticks to my face. My body shivers from the cold sweat now coating my skin as I cry out in pain once again.

"I… I don't know." I cry out, fear lacing my voice. I close my eyes as yet another spasm rocks through me. All I know is I need help, and I need it now. Suddenly, a light flashes across my closed eyes. I turn and open my eyes to see Tate turning on the lights in our room and bringing a cellphone to his ear.

"Doc, have a bed ready at the hospital now." He orders without hesitation, ending the call just as swiftly as he started it. He stuffs the device into his pocket before gently picking me up. He makes a move to leave but stops as something catches his eyes.

"Fuck." He curses, panic radiating off of him. I turn to look down at the spot I was just laying… where a spot of dark red blood greets me. Fear once again grips my heart as I clutch at my pregnant belly. I pray to all the Gods and Goddesses who may listen that my babies will be okay. Tate rushes out the house as fast as he can and places me gently into the passenger side of his Jeep, strapping me in and shutting the door in one practically seamless motion. I watch my frantic mate rush around the vehicle with panic in his eyes and settle into the driver's seat, not bothering to put on his seatbelt. He starts to speed out of the driveway.

"Hang on, Laina." He pleads through gritted teeth as I scream with pain yet again. I am grateful for being safely strapped in as Tate increases the car's speed with each and every scream and moan of pain that escapes my lips. He manages to quickly avoid wolves that cross the road, all while screaming at them to get out of the way. Fear and despair lace his voice while he assures me that everything will be okay and just to stay awake. His eyes flicker between my body that is curled in on itself and the road, his knuckles white from tightly gripping the steering wheel. The drive feels like an eternity has passed until the Jeep finally screeches to a halt in front of the building I remember to be the pack hospital. Wolves rush out to greet Tate while he rushes to my side and gingerly takes me out of the passenger seat, the smell of blood lingering in the air.

"Let's get her to an ultrasound, stat." A man says, pushing a bed towards Tate and allowing my mate to settle me onto the surface. The group of doctors and nurses rush us inside. My eyes glaze over from the pain, and all I can do is weakly hold onto Tate's hand. The next thing I know, I find myself in a large, white room, a cold gel being squirted onto my stomach while Tate holds me down. Tears escape from my eyes when I notice the nurse readying an ultrasound machine and a sinking feeling of dread weighs down my chest.

"Alpha, you need to stay calm and listen to what my team says." The man states plainly, his eyes looking sternly at Tate while a nurse does her job. My eyes wander over to a screen, the ultrasound image showing a picture of what I know to be my babies even with my blurry, tear-filled eyes.

"She is going to have to go for emergency surgery now if we are to save their lives." I hear the nurse state grimly. The scent of blood continues to grow as I feel something pierce my arm, noticing an I.V. dripping fluid into me. Soon, the medicine takes effect, and drowsiness begins to set in.

"Baby, listen to me! Everything will be fine, and when you wake up, I will be right here waiting for you." I hear Tate's voice as his fingers wipe away my tears. He kisses my lips gently and nuzzles his face into the crook of my neck. Finally, darkness takes me, and the pain disappears. I just hope that my babies are okay.

...

Beep

A soft beeping fills the room, causing annoyance to bubble inside me. The pain from earlier is finally gone and all I want is sleep.

Beep

There it goes again. I sigh, exasperated, realizing that this sound isn't going to stop until someone turns off the stupid machine making said noise.

Beep

Groaning, I open my heavy eyes and see a spotless white ceiling above me. The room is dimly lit, making the otherwise sterile room comfortable for me to open my tired eyes without flinching.

Beep

My eyes search the room for where the sound comes from.

I notice a scattering of strange machines, only to land on the one machine causing that awful noise. A stupid heartbeat monitor glares and blares back at me. I wish that someone would shut it off so that I can return to peace and quiet.

"How are you feeling, beautiful?" My head turns to a hoarse voice as I catch Tate smiling at me with relief. He looks haggard and tired with dark circles under his eyes. He scoots over on the chair he's sitting on to come closer to the bed where I lay.

"I feel numb and not as bloated. Why do I feel normal again?" I answer, a frown on my lips. My limbs refuse to move for me to rest my hand on my stomach, to feel the twins inside me, my ritual at this point. I go to turn my head, but Tate stops me, forcing me to look into his eyes.

"Before you look, listen to me." He says in a sad tone, his green eyes tearing up as a weak smile plays at his lips. A bad omen tugs at my heart as he kisses my forehead and takes a deep breath.

"The doctor tried to do everything he could. Only one of them made it." His words are soft and slow, and silence follows as they begin to sink into my hazy mind. With eyes widening and tears blurring my vision before they cascade down my face, my heart begins to break when everything settles.

I *lost* one.

My babies... and I lost one.

"Hush, Laina, it's going to be okay." Tate consoles climbing into the bed with me and wrapping me in his arms. I clutch at his shirt as I bury my face into his chest, letting out heart-wrenching sobs. All the praying I did to save my twins did nothing. One had died on me. I felt like a failure of a mother.

"W-What h-happened?" I hiccup out through my sobs pleadingly. I need to know how one of the twins died.

"The umbilical cord choked her to death. Somehow, she managed to get it wrapped around her neck, and her sister tried to help free her on instinct. That's why you bled so much." I couldn't help but feel pride for the sisterly love the two had built inside my womb, but my sobs grow, knowing that the two would never grow up together. The daydreams I pictured of two little pups chasing each other around the home Tate and I built in the last few days shattered as sadness takes hold of me. Knowing they will never grow up together breaks everything inside me. Pure sorrow fills my heart and mind. Suddenly, the sound of a tiny wail breaks my sorrowful state and brings me back to my senses. Tate sighs, brushing away the stray tears on my face and kissing my eyelids before getting up and making his way to the end of the bed. The sound of wailing comes from a wooden bassinet I hadn't noticed before. Tate reaches over and rises with a pink bundle in his arms, a soft smile on his face. He slightly bounces the fluffy bundle while making his way back to me.

"Hush, little one. Mommy just woke up and is hurting too. You'll be in her arms soon." He coos as the tiny bundle quiets slightly but continues its cries quietly.

"Is she...?" I ask hopefully, my eyes following the tiny, crying baby in his arms.

"Yes. She is your - I mean – she is our little girl." He answers with a loving smile as he passes the bundled-up baby into my waiting arms. I couldn't help but stare down at the little pup, her cries silencing as she settles into my embrace. I smiled at her, wiping tears off of her tiny little face and watching her doze off once again.

"Hi, sweetie. Welcome to the world." I whisper, gently kissing her face while Tate climbs into the bed with us. He wraps his arms around me, letting me lean into his chest as we just sit in the quiet room. Well, an almost quiet room. That stupid heartbeat monitor needs to be destroyed.

"Hello, Alpha I- oh- Luna, you're awake." A nurse said as

she approaches the room with a bottle suited for a newborn in her hand. She stops at the door, smiling at the three of us.

"I was going to come to feed the little princess, but would you like to?" She asked, coming to my side of the bed and extending the bottle towards me.

"Actually, I wanted to breastfeed her, if that's okay," I state, wanting to refuse the formula-filled bottle. I watch as the nurse sends a sympathetic smile my way as she takes one of my hands gently and places the bottle into it before backing away a respectful distance.

"Unfortunately, Luna, because of the drugs used during the operation, you will be unable to breastfeed. I'm sorry to ruin your plans." She says quietly. I nod dejectedly at her, knowing that some medications can affect the breastmilk of a nursing mother. I move the bottle to a more comfortable position in my hand, bringing the rubber nipple to my baby's lips and coax her into accepting it. I smile happily as she proceeds to drink, knowing that she will need the nutrients to grow.

"You're a natural!" The nurse states, and I smile at her enthusiasm.

"I used to babysit and help out at the pack hospital at my old Pack. I learned how to care for pups and how to coax newborns into drinking from a bottle." I answer my eyes, never leaving the pup in my arms. I could see the nurse visibly relax with my words. I knew she knew I'm sixteen and probably had a feeling that with me being so young, I wouldn't know how to raise my own child.

"That's good to know. The doctor will be in tomorrow morning, and another nurse will come to bring the next bottle when you need it. I'll leave the three of you now to enjoy the rest of your evening. Have a good night, Alpha Tate and Luna Laina." The nurse gives a respectful bow before exiting the room. Tate and I stay silent, both of us enjoying the calm night as our baby sips at her bottle. Soon, with the bottle empty and the little pup burped, Tate takes her away to have her diaper changed before placing her back into her bassinet. He crawls back into bed with me, both of us needing sleep after the last few days we've had. Snuggling into my mate's embrace, I close my eyes and let my exhausted body have the rest it needs.

CHAPTER 12

My eyes once again open to the annoying sound of the heartbeat monitor. I hate that machine with a passion as it continues to beep with my every heartbeat. Glaring at the monitor, I slowly sit up only to feel my body being pulled back down and held captive against a muscular chest.

"Where do you think you're going?" Tate mumbles, his voice husky with sleep as he nuzzles against my hair. I grin and relax against my mate, deciding to leave the grudge against the machine connected to my body.

"I was going to smash the stupid machines connected to me," I admit with the heart monitor once again beeping to punctuate my statement. I couldn't wait to get rid of these machines, especially the one with its annoying beeping. I just want to be home with Tate and our baby girl and mourn the death quietly of my other child. As if connected to my thought of her, a tiny cry of protest rings out from the bassinet. Tate groans before releasing me from his arms. He proceeds to stand from the hospital bed to gently lift the small pup from her bed. A light knock is rapt on the door before the nurse from last night walks in, giving us a quick greeting and checking over our pup before handing me a warm bottle. Taking this as our cue to feed, the little baby Tate hands her to me, still wrapped in her pink blanket, and I get to work with placing the rubber nipple to her lips and watching her latch onto it. The sound of my pup feeding fills my heart with warmth, and I take the time to just stare at her innocent little face.

"So, do you have any names for her?" Tate asks as I feed

our baby girl. I had a few, but there were two names I would want for her first and middle name.

"Julia Chris Randall-Silvermoon," I answer absent-mindedly, turning my head just far enough to see the shock on my mate's face when I say his last name.

"Why my last name?" He asks, unsure. I couldn't help but grin before I turn back to Julia. Seeing that her eyes were wide awake, staring back at me and the empty bottle, I handed the bottle to Tate and proceeded to burp her.

"You may not have sired her, but as far as she will ever know, you are her father through and through. I will not allow anyone else to raise her, but my mate, and that is you." I answer honestly, seeing the beaming smile grow radiantly as Tate comes to sit beside me and pulls me into his arms, his lips kissing my temple gently as we look down at Julia.

"I plan to name her sister Kelly Lynn Randall-Silvermoon. She needs a name to be buried with." My throat clenches with pain as a whimper escapes. I could still feel the shattering pain that comes with Kelly dying before even having a chance to live. What I would do to turn back time and have the girls born just a day earlier to prevent this tragedy, but I know I can't. I would have to live knowing that I now have a little angel living with my parents in the Goddess' court. Calloused hands wipe away stray tears that fall from my eyes.

"May I ask why Kelly?" Tate questions gently, his hands drawing soothing circles on my arms.

"She is named after my great grandmother. I remember her being kind and caring when I was a pup, and I hope that she can take care of her namesake with my parents where ever their souls are." I answer. I feel my arms slowly growing tired in their position of holding Julia, watching her little eyes slowly close. She is adorable when sleepy, and I wish I could take a picture and send it to Chris.

"Let me see our little Julia," Tate whispers, his hands moving from around me to in front as he lifts our now sleeping baby from my arms.

"Hey!" I protest, trying to reach out and take her back from Tate, only for my mate to elude my reaching hands and gently rock Julia in his arms.

"Hush, babe, Julia is sleeping." He scolds me with a playful frown on his face. I watch as he takes her to a table, seeing his quick hands change her diaper before shaking my head helplessly and lean back in the pillows. I watch silently as Tate cleans up Julia without waking her before returning her to her bassinet and joining me in bed. As he settles in and wraps me once more in his embrace, a knock on the door sounds before opening. A man in a lab coat appears in the entryway with a friendly smile on his face.

"How are my patients today?" The man asks, walking towards my bed and nodding respectfully at Tate and me. A clipboard is held in his left hand while he fumbles in his right pocket before procuring a pen and clicking it open.

"Well, Julia is fast asleep, and Laina here is comfortable. I think the machines have her annoyed." Tate answers, causing the man I now know as my Doctor to look quizzically at us.

"That's our pup. Yes, I am comfortable, and yes, I am ready to destroy the machines hooked up to me, especially this stupid heart monitor." I answer the Doctor, turning my head to glare at the heart monitor as it makes an especially loud beep. The doctor chuckles for a moment at my statement and writes notes in my file. I could see the amusement in his eyes before he turns to quickly scan Julia. I swear if I didn't place my hand on Tate's leg, he would have growled and bared his claws at the doctor, who is only doing his job.

"Both of you seem to be doing well, and my estimation right now before I do a check-up is that you will be able to go home tomorrow at the latest." I smile at the Doctor's words, excitement filling me at the prospect of going. I want to leave this hospital with its sterile smell. I want to be at home with the scent of Tate wrapping around me in our comfortable bed and the smell of breakfast as we sit in our breakfast nook.

"I am Altrex, the pack's Doctor, but everyone calls me Doctor Rex." Doctor Rex introduces himself as he comes to stand on the other side of my bed, away from Tate. I could tell my mate's protective side is taking over as his arms tighten slightly around me, and he constantly glances at our sleeping pup.

[I can't wait to get you two home safe.] He grumbles into our link, causing a bemused smile to spread across my face while he nuzzles into my neck. Men, they could be jealous monsters at the most random of times.

"Now I have to check your cuts and stitches and do a few more tests to make sure you are healing fine. Tate, if you don't mind, I need you to let Laina go so that we can see how well she is healing." Doctor Rex states with his own bemused expression. I could tell right away these two are friends as Tate grumbles incoherent words, which I believe are curses towards the Doctor before he gives me a kiss on my cheek and releases me. I watch Tate stand only to hover close to the edge of the bed, causing me to roll my eyes while I slowly sit up.

Doctor Rex performs the usual checks from listening to my lungs and heart – although the stupid heart monitor is still beating at a steady rhythm – to taking my temperature and blood pressure. After going through the motion, I am told to lie down and raise my shirt just enough for him to see my incisions from the emergency surgery. I turn my head, looking away and into Tate's eyes, not wanting to look at my flat stomach right now while Doctor Rex skims over the stitches and takes note of what he sees in my file.

"I have some good news. After checking everything over, I believe you can head home tonight." Doctor Rex announces before mentioning I can fix my shirt and sit up once again. Tate helps me straighten out clothes and supports my upper body as I slowly sit up once again before my mate joins me in bed and pulls me into his arms.

"Your incisions are healing faster than I thought, but for the next two weeks at least, you are to be on bed rest. This means no running, shifting, exercising or heavy lifting. Just relax with little Julia and laze about all day." Doctor Rex continues with a smile. The thought of being in my own bed tonight brings a smile to my face while I take a deep breath.

"Okay, Doc, I'll behave." I agree, snuggling into Tate and yawning.

"I will prescribe you some pain meds to help with the pain, but in about two weeks, you should be back to normal." With that, the Doctor left, and I smile, getting closer to Tate. A nurse comes in and unhooks my body from the multiple machines but the I.V. drip. Finally, the stupid beeping from the heart monitor is gone, and exhaustion claims me once again.

"Why don't you take a nap, beautiful. Tonight, we will be home and sleeping." Tate suggests, kissing my cheek gently and running his fingers through my hair.

"Okay," I yawn out, closing my eyes. Doctor Rex did put me on bed rest, and I plan to get as much sleep as I can while tending to Julia.

...

"For Goddess' sake, give me the car seat, Tate," I growl out in frustration, throwing my hands in the air. We have just pulled into our driveway after Julia and I were released from the hospital about an hour ago, and Tate decided to leave any form of lifting to him. The pack hospital sent us home with many bags full of newborn equipment from bottles and formulas to a blanket that my nurse – Nurse Abigail – had bought as a gift to us, her Alpha and Luna. I knew the car seat would be alright for me to carry, but my protective mate refused to let me do it.

"I got everything its fine, Laina," Tate assures through clenched teeth. I roll my eyes as I hover around the car seat with Julia inside, oblivious to her parent's arguments.

"Clearly, you don't, with how you're gritting your teeth." I retort by rolling my eyes and placing my hands on my hip. He pauses to glare at me slightly for a moment, and I glare back.

"Don't sass me, Laina. Get the door for me instead." He growls out, motioning with his head towards our front door. I scurry around him as quickly as I could and rush to turn the door knob to our house before holding it open for Tate to somehow manage to squeeze into the frame with a smug grin.

"I told you I could do it." My mate gloats with smugness in his voice. I once again roll my eyes at his childish behaviour while I close the door. Tate places the bags down gently before settling the car seat on the floor. I walk into his open arms for a hug and take a deep breath. It felt good to be home again. Pulling away from me and placing a chaste kiss on my lips, Tate turns to unstrap Julia from the car seat, a smile on his face as he holds the sleeping newborn gently in his arms.

"Come on, princess, let's get you to bed." He coos, turning to give me a quick peck on the cheek, then makes his way towards the stairs. Confused by his words, I follow Tate up the stairs wondering where his destination is.

"Tate, we haven't created a nursery yet," I say, furrowing my brows. How could we put Julia to bed when we have yet to finish the preparation for our pup? Tate just looks at me with eyes that suggest he is hiding something from me as he winks playfully, not bothering to answer my question. We continue towards the second floor and past my office coming to a stop in front of a closed door situated directly across from our own room. I knew this room well, considering this is where we had placed all the furniture and nursery items inside, intending to use this room for our pups – for Julia now that we only have her left.

"Care to open the door for us?" Tate asks cheerily, a grin spreading across his face. I roll my eyes and step forwards to turn the handle and push the wooden door. My eyes widen when I take in the scene before me. The walls were decorated with many soft colours designed to be a fairy tale forest scene in the light of the setting sun. The furniture chosen during my shopping trip with Eeva is built and set up around the room, ready to be used. The diaper changing station holds a basket with each needed item ready and in reach. My favourite item, the rocking chair, is placed beside yet another bay window where I can rock Julia asleep and sip an herbal tea. I can't help but look on in awe. This is my dream nursery.

"I told you, Tate, that if you left the design for this room to me, Laina would love it." A familiar voice says bemusedly. I turn to face the direction the voice came from only to see my cousin Chris leaning against the wall behind me, a grinning Tate standing off to the side as he looks on happily. Without a second thought, I rush into the arms of Chris, burying my face into his chest as his arms wrap around me.

"Hey, Lainy. I missed you." Chris whispers, his shoulders shaking and voice cracking. I nod in reply as sobs wrack my body. It's been over four - almost five - months since I had last seen Chris. I could remember the tears on his face as the car drove away when being designated Breeder. Now I could finally be reunited with my best friend, the person I confide in. I am finally reunited with my cousin. Slowly, my tears come to an end, and I am left gasping for breath, finding myself on the ground with my cousin holding me.

"Better?" Chris asks, wiping tears from my cheek. I could only manage a nod while my emotions stabilize. I had missed Chris so much, wanting to explain everything that's happened since leaving the pack. But Chris only kept our few calls short once I had bought my new cell phone, not wanting to have too much information in case Sam tried to use it for his own gain.

"I am so proud of you, Laina. You stayed strong and managed to free yourself." Chris whispers, kissing my forehead and giving me one last hug. I crawl out of his lap to allow Chris to stand before taking his outstretched hand and letting my cousin help me to my feet.

"How are you here?" I question once I feel confident to speak without crying again.

"Tate called me. News had spread in the old pack that you had run into this territory beforehand. When he called, I was terrified, but I felt so relieved when he told me that you are his mate. After that, Jack and I packed up the house and everything in it and moved here. I knew you would be safe by your mate's side and could finally find you. When we arrived at the house, Jack and I met Eeva. She told us about what happened, and the three of us decided to clean the house and prepare the nursery with how you had designed it in your sketchbook." He explains, a smile on his face as Chris turns to look into the nursery. I follow his gaze to catch Tate rocking our pup in his arms.

"Thank you for this." I smile, turning to thank my cousin. I needed this surprise seeing a room designed the way I had sketched out years ago. Chris nods with a soft smile, motioning me to go to my mate, who settles a sleeping Julia into her bassinet, a tender smile on his face as he gazes down at the pup before him. My legs carry me until my arms wrap around Tate from behind.

"Thank you for allowing my cousin here," I whisper, burying my face into his back and taking in his scent.

"You're welcome beautiful. I figured having your family here would help." He says, pulling me to his side. For a moment, we take in the silence of the house while gazing at Julia. It felt right having her home and asleep safe and sound.

"I hope I am not interrupting anything, but dinner is ready." Jack's familiar voice has me turning in time to catch Jack wrap his arms around Chris and give my cousin a loving kiss. It felt like the old days when I would be deep into my design homework for the two to interrupt me and force me to take a rest and eat.

"That's good because I am starving." I laugh out loud, pulling Tate along with me to where Chris and Jack stood. It felt nice knowing I would be able to taste Jack's cooking again. The four of us leave Julia to sleep and make our way down the stairs and towards the kitchen.

"Sit down. Your Aunt and Uncle are coming down to eat now." I hear the distinct tone of Eeva's voice when rounding the corner of the hall and walking into a lively scene of Eeva and a man trying to corral the pups Jonathan, Andy, and Vinny into the breakfast nook. I couldn't help but chuckle at the two chasing the three boys around while threatening to take away their games and toys.

"Laina, hi!" Eeva stops her pursuit of her pups to rush over and pull me into a hug. Her hands pat my shoulders gently with a grin plastered on her face.

"Oh, thank the Goddess that you're alright." She rushes to say with relief, her eyes scanning me from head to toe before stealing me from Tate and settling me into a chair at the breakfast nook.

"We thought to make some comfort food after the last few days you've had, so Jack suggested bacon mac n' cheese." The man states when he manages to settle the three rambunctious boys down.

"I am Loren, by the way, Eeva's mate." Loren introduces himself holding his hand out for me to shake. Smiling, I take his hand and shake it, watching Eeva curl into his side with a childish grin on her face.

"I'm Laina, Ta-"

"Tate's mate and my new Luna, we all know who you are now." He states with a playful wink. I could tell right away that I am going to like having Loren around.

"Welcome to the family."

"Thanks, Loren." I chuckle out. Soon everyone is seated with a plate full of the carb-tastic concoction that Jack whipped up. The house felt warm and lively, with my family sitting around me. We spend the meal sharing stories of our childhood laughing.

"She didn't?" Eeva asks in disbelief.

"She did. She walked up to the kid and smashed her cupcake in the poor kid's face all because he called her adorable." Jack says, and I glare at him. He is talking about the time I met one of Chris's friends from another pack as that friend's younger brother proceeded to treat me like a damsel in distress.

"In my defence, I was training to be a deadly fighter," I say matter-of-factly as I take an angry bite of the gooey, cheesy dish. I was thirteen when this happened, and I remember wanting to be a Warrior at the time, to fight and protect the pack. What a joke my loyalty turned out to be in the end.

"The best part is she then proceeds to cry because she no longer had a cupcake." Chris finishes the story causing everyone around the table to roar with laughter. I grumble into the remaining food on my plate before getting up to clear the table now that everyone is done eating.

"Nu-uh Laina, you're on bed rest, so I have this," Eeva says. Her kids have already finished eating now, Jack leading them into the living room to set up a Disney movie for the three to watch while Loren and Eeva clear the table, and Tate pulls me down to sit back and relax. Jack returns ten minutes later just as Eeva and Loren finish loading the dishwasher and return to the table, each carrying a big pastry box.

"Since everyone is finished eating, it's time for dessert," Eeva states, taking the lid off the boxes to reveal a box full of Danishes and a box full of jumbo Cupcakes. I reach for a vanilla cupcake loaded with sprinkles in and on the frosting, sinking my teeth into the delicious treat. We continue to tell stories about how Eeva and Loren found out about the two of them being mates and some about Tate as a child courtesy of Eeva. We plan to take our conversation to the living room when the tiny cries of Julia interrupt us.

"Let me go get my little niece." Eeva volunteers before disappearing from our sites. Loren chuckles and looks at Tate and me apologetically.

"She wants to try for a daughter soon, so she has baby fever right now." He explains, causing Tate to groan. Moments later, Eeva appears with Julia in her arms.

"She is adorable!" My sister-in-law gushes, her eyes never leaving Julia's tiny face.

"What is her name?" Loren asks, going to stand by his mate to peer down at my pup.

"Julia Chris Randall-Silvermoon," Tate answers, and I smile.

"Julia as in your mother's name?" Chris asks, looking at me with a grin.

"Yes, and Chris as in you," I answer my cousin, watching his eyes widen for a brief moment before he stretches out his arms expectantly at Eeva.

"Give me my new cousin." He says to Eeva only for the latter to turn away from Chris and hold Julia closer to her body.

"Get a bottle ready, and you can feed her." She states, and I smirk as my cousin gets up, gets a bottle ready and takes my pup from her before sitting back down beside Jack. I watch the two men become captivated by my little girl, their eyes never leaving her face. It would be nice if they could adopt a pup of their own soon. The two men take turns feeding and burping Julia, giving Tate and I a chance to cuddle while our family showers our pup with love and affection. I couldn't help but smile, watching everyone. Julia will definitely be spoiled as she grows.

"We bury Kelly, her twin sister, tomorrow," I announce quietly as I now hold a sleeping baby in my arms. The room grows silent with this information.

"We will be there," Loren speaks up, giving me a small smile as everyone else in the room agrees. I nod and smile sadly as I snuggle into Tate, yawning.

"I think it's time for everyone to sleep." Tate chuckles, rubbing my back gently and causing my eyes to grow heavy.

"Yeah, we should get these children to bed now. Good night." Eeva agrees as Loren heads into the living room to gather the boys. When they leave, Chris and Jack head into the guest room that I once occupied. With the house settling in silence and Julia once again fast asleep in her own room, I settle into bed with Tate curling into his arms and quickly falling asleep. I missed being home.

CHAPTER 13

"You ready?" Tate's voice floats to me, and I sigh, taking a last look at myself in the mirror. My blue eyes held unshed tears in them once again as sorrow fills me. I stand wearing a long-sleeved black lace dress with my hair in a high bun. Today will be a long and depressing day for everyone. I feel strong arms turn me away from my pale reflection and press my head into a sturdy chest as I take in Tate's scent with a shaky breath.

"You don't have to go if it's too hard, Laina. Everyone would understand." He says and kisses my forehead. He knew I am close to breaking again. Any mother would be close to breaking on the day they burry their baby.

"I have to, Tate. She deserves to know how much I love her and will miss her." I whisper out with a whimper into his chest. Taking another deep breath to steady my emotions, I take Tate's hand, and the two of us make our way down the stairs where Jack and Chris fawn over Julia, a soft smile on my lips as I watch the three of them.

"Who is a fabulous little baby? You are, yes, you are little Julia. And your big cousins here are going to make sure you stay fabulous with clothes fit for this little princess." Chris coos as he taps gently on Julia's tiny nose. I knew what he is saying will come true and that, like myself, Julia will be showered with clothing growing up. I feel Tate stiffen beside me as Chris bounces Julia in his arms as he talks about all the things she will get growing up and what she might become in the future, causing my mate to growl lowly where only I can hear it. I knew Tate is extremely possessive, and I guess with Chris acting this way, maybe he felt his position threatened.

"Behave, Tate. Chris and Jack are always like this, especially Chris. He means no harm." I sigh out, wrapping my arm around Tate's waist and trying to calm my mate down as best as I can. Instead of calming down, Tate rolls his eyes and continues to glare at Chris, pulling away from me. Hurt fills my already bruised heart at my mate's reaction. Trying to calm myself down, I turn away from Tate and shy away from his touch when he reaches for me. I walk towards Chris and Jack taking Julia from Chris's arms and cradle her as I breathe in her baby scent.

"Julia and I are riding in your car, Chris." I decide, hearing Tate give a low, possessive growl. I turn to glare at my mate. Today is already a hard-enough day for me, and I will not allow his attitude to take over and hurt me even more emotionally.

"Wouldn't you rather be with Tate?" Jack asks cautiously, his eyes darting between Tate and I.

"No. I would rather ride with family than be stuck in a car with a possessive ass that can't control his attitude today." I answer honestly. I bend down to place Julia in her car seat, watching Jack carefully pick it up. Chris grabs Julia's diaper bag getting ready to leave.

"Why are you being so difficult? A moment ago, you were ready to cry, and now you're acting like a class "A" bitch!" Tate growls, directing his anger towards me. My heart cracks slightly as a few tears slip out from the corner of my eyes, and I shake my head at Tate.

"I'm only acting like this because of you." I snap back at Tate, watching as his eyes widen in shock.

"Here, Chris is being not only a cousin but also an uncle to Julia, and you get jealous of him. He's gay and has a mate, but just because you feel slightly threatened, you start growling and being an asshole. Today is not the day to do this, Tate. I am burying one of my pups. Do you understand the pain I am in?" I continue, more tears streaming down my face as Chris holds his arm out, preventing me from going to where I left Tate and slapping some sense into him.

"Chris is my best friend. When my parents died, he raised me. So, excuse me for taking my family's side when my mate starts acting like a grade-A douchebag." I finish my rant and turn on my heels and proceed to drag Chris to his car. I needed to be away from Tate for a moment. Jack follows suit and helps me secure Julia and her car seat in the back seat before the three of us settle into the car ourselves.

"Just drive, Chris." I sigh, seeing the hesitation in my cousin's eyes for leaving Tate in the house alone. *When my mate smartens up, then I will talk to him. But today is not the day to act the way he is.* The engine starts, and Chris proceeds to back out of the driveway. My eyes stay focused on Julia beside me as I wipe away the wetness on my face.

The drive to the church is short as we pass through the forest roads. The trees shake, and leaves break off, falling to the ground. I take the time and try my best to compose myself as Chris parks in front of a gorgeous, white brick church that Eeva told me was built over one hundred years ago. It was gorgeous, and the cloudless blue sky provided a lovely scene. For such a sad day, it was beautiful out. Maybe the Moon Goddess felt sorry for me losing my pup Kelly and provided a beautiful scene to send her off. Chris comes to the side Julia's car seat is secured in and offers to carry her inside. I reach for the diaper bag, but Jack grabs it before I can, giving me a side hug and a kiss on my forehead. It made me happy having these two here. We make our way into the church's opened double doors when a wolf in a long robe steps forward from the dais and gives me a warm smile.

"Luna, so nice to meet you, but I am sad that it had to be under these circumstances." The minister greets, offering his hand for me to shake. I smile sadly and look around the room, my eyes searching for Kelly's body.

"I-is she?" I couldn't help but let a few more tears fall as I ask. I wanted to see her for the first and last time.

"She is in the other room; would you like some time with her?" The minister asks with a sympathetic gaze. I nod slowly, motioning for him to lead the way while Jack and Chris smile reassuringly at me and takes Julia to the front pew to entertain the newborn. I am led to a room to the left of the stage where a wooden table with a black satin table cloth stands. On top of the table is a small wooden casket with white satin that cradles the body of a tiny newborn, who is a carbon copy of Julia. The minister leaves, closing the door behind him while I slowly walk forward until I stand before Kelly, my fingers grazing her small cheeks gently.

"Hi, Kelly." I choke out as tears once again flow down my face. Something compels me to gently lift her lifeless body in my arms as sobs begin to take hold of me. I fall to my knees while staring at the still face of my baby girl. Here I am, holding onto Kelly, the pup who used to kick inside me just days ago, and I would never get to watch her grow up. She couldn't feel my touch or be comforted in my arms. She'll never grow up with Julia.

"I love you, baby girl," I whisper, kissing her sweet little face, my tears falling onto her pale little cheeks. I sit in the small, quiet room, just holding onto Kelly and slightly rocking back and forth. I wish I could turn back time, so this day never happens.

"Laina?" Eeva calls out to me gently. I turn my head to look at my friend, watching her take slow steps to stand before me, a sad smile on her face as she holds out her hands.

"It's time. May I take her?" She informs, asking me gently about Kelly. I hesitate for a moment before nodding, allowing Eeva to take Kelly from my arms. Eeva gently places Kelly into her coffin. She rearranges her pink dress so that it sits elegantly on my pup's body as more sobs come from me.

"Ssshh, it'll be okay," Eeva whispers, taking a seat beside me on the ground and wrapping her arms around me. I bury my face into my friend's shoulder and allow myself to grieve for my pup, who I will never watch grow up, who will never run around with her sister. For a while, the two of us stay in this position as Eeva allows me to cry, my sobs slowing down until I am able to catch my breath. She takes out cleansing wipes from her purse and helps me clean my face, squeezing my hands gently before helping me to my feet. I turn to look at Kelly one last time, re-arranging her dress and taking a small headband I had made last week. It was a black band with fall flowers and a colourful butterfly. Julia is already wearing the matching headband, and it felt right to let Kelly wear her own headband today.

"Goodbye, sweet girl," I whisper, giving her a final kiss on her tiny forehead before Eeva leads me out of the room gently. Walking back into the central part of the church, I catch Tate in the back talking to the minister but ignore him. Instead, I join Chris and Jack in the front, taking Julia from Jack's arms and holding my baby close to me. We all take a seat on the benches as the minister starts his speech about the balance of life and the blessing from the Goddess, Loren and Jack carrying the tiny coffin to the front where everyone I knew could see her. I already had my moment, so I just stare at Julia, not wanting to see the small coffin. Someone slides into the spot next to me, strong arms wrapping around me and pulling close.

"Laina, I...I'm sorry. I was an ass this morning." It was Tate, and those few words are all I need to turn into his chest and cry silently, careful not to wake our sleeping pup in my arms. The rest of the funeral is a blur. The only thing I remember is the coffin being lowered and buried in the tomb where Tate's family is buried. She will forever be a Randall-Silvermoon and Tate's pup no matter what.

I don't remember how I ended up in bed curled under the covers, but I know that Tate allowed Chris and Jack to care for Julia for the night. I needed some time alone after the long, heart-wrenching day I've had. I knew Tate was in his office, but he would check in on me every now and then. With my body feeling zapped of all energy, I decided to close my heavy eyelids and let sleep welcome me.

CHAPTER 14

Light slowly drifts in through the sheer curtains, falling across my eyelids, causing me to wake up. Strong arms are wrapped around me with my back against a sturdy chest. The tingles against my skin tell me that it's Tate as he snuggles closer to me. I needed to get my mind off of yesterday and move forward. I will always love Kelly, but Julia needed her mother to raise her. Today is a new day, and slowly my grief will settle down.

Tate slowly pulls away from me and kisses my forehead before his presence leaves the bed. Ten minutes pass by till I decide that I did not want to stay here in bed forever, and I throw the covers back to stand. Stretching, I make my way towards the bathroom for a shower, letting the warm water cleanse away the smell of grief from yesterday off of my body. I feel more refreshed as I shut off the water and wrap my body in a fluffy towel, still learning to get used to my small stomach once again. I step away from the master en-suite and pad towards the closet towel, drying my hair. Something about a morning shower always made me feel lighter and energetic. Dressing in a shortfall dress, I braid my hair and make my way downstairs and towards the smell of breakfast cooking in the kitchen.

"Come here, princess!" I hear Tate's voice before seeing him and everyone else as I round the corner to the kitchen entrance just in time to watch Jack pass Julia to my mate.

"Good morning," I say, smiling as I walk towards them, kissing my mate on the cheek before taking Julia from him.

Hey we were having daddy-daughter time!" He exclaims while I sit down on a chair with her in my arms across from my mate.

"New-born babies are cute but boring," Jack says with a sigh. I fake gasp at him, shielding Julia from Jack's sight and shaking my head at my cousin-in-law.

"Shame on you. She is busy being adorable." I say in mock scolding before kissing my pup gently on her little nose.

"Yes, she is, and you need to be busy eating," Tate says. I smile when my mate places a plateful of food in front of me, with a glass of orange juice. But I protest when he takes Julia away from me.

"Hey, I had her!" I exclaim, reaching out to take our pup away from him again.

"And now you are eating." He smirks, and I glare at him as he takes Julia back to his seat.

"She may not be my flesh and blood, but the moment I saw her, I knew she would be my little girl." He says, smiling, and I couldn't help but smile at his declaration as I give in and begin to eat.

The four of us enjoy the quiet morning, taking turns passing Julia around and taking pictures with her. I smile when Chris and Jack announce that they are looking at adopting their own pup soon once they settle into their own house here in Bloodsvain. It felt like life was finally set on the right track for my family and me.

Suddenly, everything turns into chaos as wolves in uniforms worn by the Council of Elders storm into the kitchen, the sounds of glass shattering from the windows breaking open. Julia is placed into my arms with Tate backing me into a wall, taking a protective stance in front of us, a threatening growl rolling over the crowd.

"Laina Starcrest, you are under arrest for kidnapping!" A man states as he steps forward, weary of Tate. I could tell he did not want to go against my mate, and I had a feeling he would lose if Tate attacks.

"Tate Randall-Silvermoon, step down. This she-wolf stole a pup from Samuel from Pine-" I growl loudly, cutting the man off as I send a vicious glare his way.

"I did no such thing. This is my pup, and she was born a few days ago along with her twin, whom we just buried yesterday." I snap, holding my baby closer to my chest, protecting her. I hated these men who invaded my house and threatened to take my pup away from me.

"Alpha Sam said you would say that, but he has documents for a baby boy born two weeks ago." The man states, taking out what looks to be a copy of fake documents. Sam must have been prepared to fight for these pups, but too bad for him. He will never hold a claim to Julia.

"Look closely, idiot, my mate is holding a baby girl!" Tate roars, and everyone freezes, the men sniffing the air. The man in front of Tate looks at him in confusion before peering over his shoulder towards me.

"It seems that you are speaking the truth. What were the elders thinking?" The man I now assume is the leader states as he catches a glimpse of Julia. I turn my body so that my back faces the men, guarding my pup from their gazes and sending a glare in their direction.

"I'll tell you what they were thinking. They weren't!" I growl out in anger. The leader looks at us again, but I keep his curious gaze off of Julia. He has no right to see her.

"How about we talk this out at the head office? My crew will fix up your house. Sorry, by the way." The man concedes with a shrug, getting ready to turn away.

"Sorry! YOU'RE SAYING SORRY WHEN YOU CAME IN TO TAKE MY MATE!" Tate roars as he charges the man, pinning him to a wall with his hands around his neck, his face set in rage as he chokes the man. Some of the wolves rush to Tate's side, working hard to loosen my mate's grip around their leader's neck only to be elbowed or headbutted out of the way by a very pissed-off, protective Alpha. They fucked with the wrong wolf today. I sigh and hand Julia to Jack before walking over and placing a hand on Tate's cheek, seeing his eyes turn to me as he releases a growl.

"Tate, calm down," I say calmly, trying to ease his hands away from the wolf's neck.

"NO, I WILL N'-"

"You can, and you will." I let authority into my voice while my blood simmers with the power I rarely use. He blinks a couple of times, probably surprised at my command before staring at me.

"Tate, please." He growls once more and finally lets go with a huff of breath before throwing the leader of the guards to the ground with a loud, sickening thud, causing me to wonder if the leader broke a couple of bones in the process. Tate glares at the man before backing away and heading towards Julia, carefully taking our pup from Jack and holding our baby in his arms. I watch as he visibly relaxes and smiles gently. Tate fully accepts Julia as his pup, and it makes me so happy. Knowing my mate will be fine, I turn on my heel and glare at the man, who is now gasping for air, as I walk towards him and lean down so that my face is an inch away from him, letting the power of my blood wash over his frame. I watch him stiffen with fear as I look into his eyes, my own anger radiating off of me.

"Now, you will get the Elders to come HERE, or I will call the Alpha King and have HIM deal with this issue. Do I make myself clear?" I emphasize a few words, and the man nods, getting his phone out and dialling a number quickly. My eyes never leave him, and I watch him visibly shudder. If he thought Tate is scary to deal with, he has never faced a pissed-off mother werewolf who is willing to kill anyone who threatens her pups.

"Elder Ross, it seems like the information given to us was incorrect, and because of the way we handled things, they want you and the others to come here... Of course... Got it, see you then." He hangs up and leans against the wall breathing heavily as sweat drips down his forehead

"Two hours. They will be here in two hours." He answers, and I stand, letting the pressure ease off of him.

"Good, your men can fix my house now while we wait for their arrival," I order, giving each of them a glare. No one protests, knowing this mistake is their fault, as every wolf readies themselves to repair the damages they have done. I needed to talk to Tate about added security to our home to protect Julia and any other pups we will have. I sigh and turn towards Tate, seeing that he has one arm open while looking at me. I smile and take the few steps into his embrace as he holds Julia and me.

"Now you can tell them what happened to you." I nod at his words and press my face into his chest and take in his scent.

"Well, Jack and I will make sure the house gets fixed properly. You two go relax with Julia and wait for the Elders to arrive," Chris volunteers giving us an exasperated sigh as he looks around at the mess. I knew my cousin would make these wolves work like slaves for what they did. Chris could be sadistic when pissed off, and I can see the rage simmering behind his eyes. Thanking Chris, Tate leads me away from the kitchen and out the sliding door onto our deck. Thinking we are stopping here, I get ready to rest on a patio chair, only for Tate to grab my wrist and lead me away from the house.

"Why are we going here?" I ask, curiosity filling my voice. Today is unusually warm for a late September morning, and part of me worries that Julia will get cold if she is out here for too long.

"It's a surprise." He answers with a mischievous grin. We walk hand-in-hand for a few minutes into the forest, just past our house, when the sounds of waves reach me. Suddenly, Tate stops and blocks my view, smiling at me, a now sleeping Julia resting in the crook of his right arm.

"Ready?" He asks, and I giggle. I could tell he has planned this surprise for a while, and I couldn't wait to see it.

"Yes!" I answer, getting a wink before he moves aside. I gasp as I see a beautiful white gazebo resting on a huge pond as if it were floating on the water. Water lilies float across the water, and large, smooth, circular stones large enough to fit two people at a time create a pathway to the gazebo. My feet carry me from stone to stone until I find myself at the entrance to the beautiful place. A small fireplace radiates heat around the area, causing me to smile at the coziness while taking a seat on one of the comfortable chairs. Tate places our sleeping pup in a bassinet, covering her with a blanket, before taking a seat next to me. We gaze out across the pond.

"And now, we wait for the Elders to arrive," Tate whispers as a few ducks swim by.

CHAPTER 15

"It's been two hours. Where are they?" Tate asks no one in particular as he paces around the gazebo while I feed Julia. We spent two hours enjoying the view and having a light snack while we wait. Chris would update me every now and then talk about the repairs to our house, but I had a feeling he was enjoying being a dictator to the wolves who crashed in unwelcomed.

"Alpha Tate and Luna Laina?" I jumped slightly when a voice calls out to us and turn to spot a wolf dressed in our pack formalwear.

"I was told to inform you that the Elders are here. Do you want them to be led to the gazebo?" The man asks. He turns away from Tate to look at me, giving me a friendly smile and causing Tate to growl possessively. The wolf looks away quickly and bows his head submissively.

"Sorry, Alpha I just wanted to introduce myself to the Luna. I am the Head Warrior here and in charge of protection. We've also doubled security patrols since this morning's incident." The wolf explains, not moving from his bowed position. Tate growls again, and I roll my eyes, giving my mate a pointed look.

"Tate, behave. He isn't a threat," I warn as I stand, placing Julia in her bassinet before walking forward to shake this new wolf's hand.

"I'm Laina," I say, smiling, having to step back to take a good look at this wolf.

"Mike." He replies with laughing. What is with the guys

here being six feet or over? I smile back at Mike and return to Tate's side, kissing my mate on his cheek.

"Bring the Elders here and have someone bring snacks and drinks as well," Tate says once I am safely in his arms. I know he is a little on edge since this morning and decide to play it safe and stay in reach of his arms.

"I hate it when guys look at you. You're mine." He growls to himself, holding me possessively. I sigh again and get onto my tiptoes, kissing his jaw gently. I tell him I feel the same way when females stare at him and remind him that Mike works as one of the top members of the pack and will not harm me. After sucking up to Tate and reassuring him that I am his and his only, I finally get a chuckle from my mate.

"Let's go sit and wait," I suggest, and he nods, leading me back to the seats we vacated. His hand grasps mine as he draws little circles on the back of my hand. He brings my hand up to his lips every now and then for a kiss.

"When they come, let me talk," I say. It is my story and problem to talk about, and I felt better speaking up for myself. I watch Tate's eyes stare at the water as he thinks about letting me talk. I wait patiently for him to speak, sipping on my tea and relaxing into the chair as the wind flutters by.

"Fine, but if I feel that your life and Julia's is in danger, then I step in." He agrees after a few minutes pass. I could tell letting me take the spotlight worries him, but it had to be done.

"Okay, deal!" I smile and kiss Tate happily, liking the fact that my mate is giving me a chance to take the lead on this situation before settling down once again in my chair, my mood a little lighter. We quietly wait for our "guests" to arrive, another half an hour passing by before Mike and two Warriors lead a group of Elderly wolves towards us. Two wolves I recognize from our pack follow behind with trays of food.

The Elderly wolves cross the bridge first, sitting down

without shaking our hands or giving us a simple greeting. It took everything in me not to growl at them. The two other wolves nod at Tate and me respectfully before setting pots of tea and coffee, cups and some pastries on the table in front of us. They bow once again before leaving and passing by the two guards stationed at the shoreline. Mike stands at the entrance of the gazebo, waiting for orders and scanning his eyes over the surroundings for any threats.

"Mike, we need a witness to stay here while we converse with the Elders," Tate says through gritted teeth, his eyes glaring at the wolves who sit before us. I reach for his hand under the table and squeeze gently, knowing exactly how he feels. This is our territory, and their disrespect has us on edge more than the incident of their lackeys crashing into our kitchen.

"Yes, Alpha. It's why I have all of the appropriate equipment ready." His eyes glaze over for a moment before two more wolves appear in our line of sight. They carry what looks to be a camera set as they cross over and begin to set up the electronics, including a voice recorder, around the gazebo with precise movement. With a bow of respect to us, the wolves turn and leave the vicinity. Mike double-checks everything before sitting beside Tate.

"Now, let's get this started," I say, folding my hands neatly on the table and staring at the Elders.

"Didn't your parents tell you it's rude to stare, little girl?" The man in the middle says, and I smile sweetly at him.

"My parents couldn't teach me much because rogues killed them." They stare at me with open mouths, and I could sense that Tate is smirking and Mike is trying hard to hold back his laughter at my retort. I could tell some of the Elders hate my brutal honesty, but I could care less about their opinion of me.

"Now, why was there an arrest warrant on me?" I ask, and the Elders growl at my direct question.

"What gives you the right to demand answers?" A she-wolf visibly bristles at my questioning as she growls at my disrespect to the group. I simply send a glare her way, holding my hand out to stop Tate from doing something.

"Because Samuel Lightran forced me to be a Breeder as well as other females in my old pack and raped me to have an heir," I growl threateningly at them. Before I can continue what I want to say, the Elder in the middle stands up, slamming his hands on the table and glares at me.

"My great-great-nephew would do no such thing!" He yells quickly to defend Samuel. My eyes carefully observe this wolf as I continue my side of the events that unfolded over the last few months.

"Really, do you want proof that I got pregnant just a little over four months ago by your great-great-nephew? I ran away, wanting to protect my pups. Yes, pups as in two. A few days ago, I had to have emergency surgery due to complications, and only one pup survived. We just buried her sister yesterday only for this bullshit to happen this morning." To prove my point, a small cry is heard after my words, and Tate swiftly rises to pick up Julia and soothe her. The Elderly she-wolf who questioned me earlier takes a long look at me, her eyes holding sympathy and curiosity.

"You are Laina. Eeva said she had found a wolf who was a forced Breeder. She didn't say which pack she had run away from." She states, and I smile at her. It seems like I have found an ally in this group of Elders and decide to treat her with a little more respect. Thank you, Eeva, for reporting this through the proper channels.

"Yes, I am Laina, the she-wolf who was raped. Now I suggest you see the Pinepaw Pack unannounced, with me, Tate and Chris – my cousin and technical guardian as I am only sixteen – present so that you can see where I was kept and where other Breeders are kept," The man was still standing. I looked at him with distrust in my eyes.

"He stays out of the conversation since he could warn Sam, and then you will never know the truth," I add at the end. The man's face starts to turn red with rage, and he hits the table again, this time shattering it, as the sound of glass breaks and everything else on the table falls to the ground. I am grateful that Tate is holding Julia away from the table as I let out a low growl. This wolf is a threat to my family.

"You cannot make me do anything! If I want to be here for all the details, I will!" He roars at me, the disrespect evident in his eyes. I stand, my hand reaching out to grab the collar of his shirt as I pull him closer, my face inches from his as my canines start to grow.

"I can and I will since you are related to the man that raped me. Now, sit down, shut up, and behave. You also owe me a new table." The Elder and I had a staredown as we glared at each other. I refuse to release him, relishing in the fact that he is a foot shorter than me and a lot weaker as well. I am done being the weak pushover from a few months ago when Samuel decided to make me a breeder. I am a soon-to-be Luna and a mother. I would do whatever it takes to get justice and protect my pup.

"Ross, just sit down. We already decided to leave you out of this." The female Elder commands, and Ross looked at her with wide eyes as the two silently converse.

"You can't do that, Dian." He states and glares at her.

"I can, as the head Elder." The woman, Dian, says. I smirk in triumph, releasing Ross and sitting back down beside Tate, who has now joined us, informing me Julia is asleep once again. We watch as the elders have another conversation through their link before Ross growls in frustration and stalks away.

"Sorry about that, Laina," Dian says, and I smile at her.

"So, can we have a civil conversation now?" Tate asks, looking down at the table frame.

"Of course. We will also have a new table sent your way soon." A man to Dian's right says. And so, our conversation turns to civility while I recount the events that lead me to where we are today.

...

"Good night, sweetheart," I whisper as I lower Julia into her bed for the night. The sounds of running water could be heard from across the hall from Tate and mine's bedroom. I smile, watching my pup for a moment before heading towards my room and stretch my sore muscles.

"Time for a bit of R and R?" I groan to myself, rubbing my shoulder.

"Yes, and we are having one together tonight," Tate says, wrapping me in his embrace and kissing my forehead.

"But-" I begin, ready to protest.

"No buts, beautiful, we need some time to ourselves." Tate cuts me off, poking my nose playfully. I smile gently and nod, stepping out of his arms and undressing.

"I will only do this if you give me a massage," I state, dropping my pants and underwear onto the ground.

"Okay, deal." His voice is a whisper as he hugs me from behind once again, his body pressed to my own and completely naked. Without warning, I am scooped into his arms as Tate carries me princess-style into our large bathroom, placing me gently into the large tub filled with a bubble bath. He climbs in behind me, his hands kneading my shoulders and back, making quick work of the sore muscles I have and releasing the tension that has built up over the last few days.

"I know you're still healing from your surgery, so we will only have a bath tonight. But I can't wait to make you mine forever." He says with longing, and my heart flutters. Everyone in the pack I have met has called me Luna, but we weren't fully mated yet, and I haven't been accepted into the pack in an official ceremony yet.

"When will I become a member of the pack?" I ask after we were both scrubbed and getting out to dry off to head to bed for some much-needed sleep.

"Whenever you feel like you're ready." He answers, kissing my forehead.

"What about this Saturday? It's a full moon, and it would be a perfect time." I suggest, getting a breathtaking smile from him.

"Deal. We will do it at the pack house, and it's a week before we go to Pine Paw, so that gives you time to explore the pack territory as their Luna." He agrees, picking me up bridal style and kissing me.

"But for now, you need your sleep. So, grab one of my shirts to wear to bed while I shave." He adds, putting me on my feet again before he turns back towards the bathroom vanity, the sounds of water running, signalling he is getting ready to shave. I smile and rush to his dresser, going through the neatly stacked shirts and finding a V-neck t-shirt that matches his eye colour, hastily putting it on with a pair of plain black boyshorts, and towel-drying my hair, all before slipping under the covers. Soon, Tate comes out with a towel around his waist and heads into the closet, his face neatly shaven. He returns minutes later with pyjama pants slung over his hips loosely and shirtless, pulling me into his arms as he crawls into his side of the bed.

"Goodnight, beautiful," he whispers, kissing me gently.

"Goodnight," I whisper back, yawning as I snuggle closer to him, sleep taking over. He chuckled at how fast I am falling asleep, and I smile, opening my eyes to sneak one last look at him before I journey into dreamland.

"I love you." His voice is quieter than a whisper, but I hear those words clearly, and they stay with me as darkness fades in, and I fall asleep feeling safe and sound.

CHAPTER 16

"You look beautiful, Laina. Everyone is going to love you." Eeva praises me as I turn around in a circle, looking at myself in the mirror. Today is the day I will officially become a member of Bloodsvain. For the last two weeks, I have already considered this pack home, and now it is time for me to join. Nerves flutter around inside me as I smooth out the dress I am wearing, ensuring everything is in place before turning to face Eeva. Eeva's house is close to where the pack ceremonies take place. With Loren as the Beta, it fell under his duties to protect the sacred lake that has been used for generations in welcoming new members and new leaders.

"Are you sure? I'm sixteen. What if they don't want someone young and inexperienced for their Luna?" I ask, pacing the length of her bedroom. Part of me felt worried that the pack would resent me for being so young. Tate and I have a ten-year age gap, but I knew some couples were even many years older than the other. As werewolves, we can live for a long time due to our supernatural genes. Some mates could have an age gap as large as one hundred years between one another. It is normal. Sighing, I return to the full-length mirror and gaze at my reflection. My pale skin has turned to a healthy glow with more rest and healing. Tate made sure I rarely did any heavy lifting and even locked the workout room so I don't try to sneak in a quick workout. My hands smooth out the strapless, cream, figure-skating dress I was told to wear by Eeva. The front half of the dress falls down to mid-calf while the back half of the dress ends in a two-foot train that trails behind me. The material is light and flowing, leaving the dress to flutter in the wind when I move. My long, chestnut hair is styled in curls away from my face, and a crown of wildflowers rests on top of my head. White gold bangles adorn my wrists, and white gold armlets wrap around my forearms and upper arms, adding to the majestic feeling that I emit. Eeva took the time to paint the pack insignia on the center of my chest in dark, blood-red body paint, with golden paw prints scattered on the visible skin all over my body, as per the tradition of a new Luna.

"News has already spread about you. People can't wait to meet you and get to know you. They want you as their Luna." My friend explains with a grin on her face. I knew that Eeva had started spreading the news about Tate finding his mate and that the warriors Tate and I would cross paths with would have said a few words, so it made sense that the pack already knew about me. Personally, I was just worried about not being a good Luna.

"Besides, you're not the only one getting accepted into the pack." She continues, and I smile. Eeva is right that I wouldn't be the only one. Chris and Jack were joining the pack, and so would Julia when I join, as I am her mother. I couldn't wait to watch my baby girl grow up in a strong pack that stands together and not have to fear about becoming a Breeder. She will have endless possibilities when she shifts, and it makes my heart swell with pride thinking about it.

"Okay then, I can do this," I whisper to myself, staring into my reflection as my blue eyes twinkle. A wolf howls in the distance, causing me to jump from the sudden noise. I glare when I catch Eeva clutching at her side with laughter at my reaction. Excuse me for being jittery today.

"Are you afraid of the big bad wolf?" Eeva jokes at my expense. I just roll my eyes and walk to the table that holds a pot of tea that Eeva and I have been sipping throughout the day, lifting my glass and taking a needed drink of chamomile tea.

"Not one bit, considering that the big bad wolf is my mate." I retort, with Eeva fake-gagging at my cheeky response.

She sighs before getting to her feet and handing me a shoebox.

"Well, that was the signal for the ceremony to start. Put these on, and we can go." She explains, picking up a cookie. I slip on the white Egyptian sandals before we head downstairs and out the back door, taking a dark path into the woods. The fallen leaves crunch under my feet, and I smile at the warm fall night and the fresh, clean air in this forest. Fall is my favourite season, and as I look up at the full moon, I can't help but smile. My life is full now. I have a mate I wanted to be with, a pack I know I will love, and a beautiful pup who will hopefully have siblings in a year or two. Today will mark my beginning of forever with Tate as his Luna of the Bloodsvain wolves, and I can't wait. It feels right being here.

Eeva and I converse about upcoming events the pack holds for October, my favourite being the pumpkin carving that pups and their mothers do the day before Halloween. It felt nice knowing the pack comes together as a community for fun holiday events. The dark forest soon brightens up with lanterns hung every so often on trees until the lake comes into view. The pack is already congratulating the regular wolves who have just finished being accepted into the pack. As the Luna, it is customary for me to join the pack last during a joining ceremony, as I can connect to every current member in the pack. Tate just wanted to say he saved the best for last.

Noticing our presence, the pack turns to greet Eeva and me as they separate into two sides, opening a large path for me to walk through. As I walk past the wolves, each one bows to me respectfully. I smile at them feeling their acceptance in the air until my eyes face forwards just as the path opens up to reveal the edge of the lake illuminated by the full moon with Tate standing inside. He smiles at me, and I smile back, taking the last few steps towards him until I stood directly across from my mate in the chilly water, the moon making the water appear silvery below us.

"Today, we welcome Laina Starcrest as a new member to our pack, as my mate and as our Luna!" Tate begins, his voice loud and carrying past the group of wolves. Cheers of excitement follow his words, causing a blush to crawl along my skin. Waiting for the crowd to settle down, Tate takes the time to look into my eyes, mouthing the words 'You look beautiful" to me. When silence settles over the lake once again, he takes a deep breath.

"Laina, do you promise to uphold the laws of the pack and perform the duties of your role as a just and true Luna?" Tate continues, asking me the one question every Luna is faced with answering. I see the love and devotion behind his gaze, causing the nerves I felt earlier to turn into giddy butterflies. I have an amazing mate.

"I do," I answer confidently, conviction filling my voice. I felt whole answering Tate back, knowing that my role will always keep me beside him as we lead as equals.

"Then we welcome you to the pack as a member and our Luna." He raises his left hand, a blade in his right as he slowly cuts a line before turning the handle for me to take. I copy his movements, cutting a line into my left palm and wincing from the pain of the blade. Taking my bleeding hand, Tate grasps mine, and our blood mingles with one another. All at once, pack magic flows into me, causing my knees to buckle with its force and Tate reaching out to grasp my waist and keep me from falling. I close my eyes as the power opens up the link to the pack, many voices filling my head. I needed to wait for the magic to settle before I could close each channel off and be able to have silence once again. Taking a deep breath, with our bleeding hands still clasped, I feel Tate shift until I am leaning against him. My body shivers as the magic runs its course and settles down, allowing me to turn off the pack link and tune out the voices of the wolves I will be leading. Finally, silence resumes once again, and I open my eyes, seeing my reflection and noticing the neon blue glow. I am finally a member of Blodsvain. Cheers erupt around me, and I jump from the sudden noise. Shaking my head helplessly at the celebrating wolves, I turn to catch Tate glaring at our pack as Mike walks forward and hands us each a towel to clean our hands. The pack continues to chat loudly for a second until a loud wail sounds to the left, quieting the pack while Chris steps forward to hand me an upset Julia whose eyes still glow like mine. She and I were now members of the pack, and I was happy that, as her mother, I would be the only one who has to go through the initiation since she is still a newborn.

"We're home here in Bloodsvain," I tell her as she quiets in my arms and I walk out of the water. I watch the glow fade from her eyes, finally noticing that she has my eye colour. Tate finishes speaking with Mike and joins us on the shore, wrapping me in his embrace and kissing me passionately in front of everyone. I could feel the promise in his kiss that soon we will be fully mated, and I couldn't wait for that day to come.

Flames catch my attention when I pull away breathlessly from my mate. Bonfires were lit up just a few feet away in the clearing beside the lake, and the smell of food wafts towards everyone in the wind. Taking my hand, Tate and I lead the pack to celebrate. I smile and laugh as I get to know my new pack mates while Tate finds excuses to fill my plate with food. Julia is carried away by Eeva, Chris and Jack as the three, thick as thieves, explain that she needs to learn about her territory as Tate and my pup. Every now and then, Tate would bring her back only for one of them to steal her again, but I knew she is safe. She is surrounded by her family, and each member probably feared what would happen to them if something happens to Julia. They knew how vicious and blood-thirsty Tate could be, but they would soon learn what I could do if my pup is harmed. The moon is high in the sky, and Julia sleeps in a baby carriage. Tate and I decide to end the celebration and allow everyone to go home to sleep. We were saying our farewells for the night, exhaustion settling in, when loud howls meant to signify a war cry sound out.

I freeze with fear. I know those howls all too well.

"Is that rogues?" Someone asked, and I shake my head, turning to look at Tate with fear.

"Pine Paw," I whisper, picking Julia up and clutching her to my body, careful not to wake her.

"CHRIS! JACK!" He yells as I feel two pairs of hands grab me, with my cousin and his mate on either side, ready to protect Julia and me.

"All pregnant wolves, pups and mothers to the shelter. Ten warriors go to protect them and my mate and pup. Chris and Jack stay with her. Any able-bodied wolf ready to fight, follow me. Anyone who cannot fight is expected to head into the shelters as well. Stay safe, everyone." My mate orders before taking my face in his hands and kissing me. This one was different than before. It was needy and filled with emotion, but it ended too quickly before I am whisked away with Tate and other wolves rushing towards the sounds of the howls.

[I love you!] His voice fills my head, and then it's gone. He cut the pack link from me no matter how many times I reached out to him. He is in Alpha mode, and only the battle to protect his pack matters right now.

Before I knew it, I found myself in the pack house being led into the kitchen where the large pantry is wide open. A section of the back wall is pulled away, revealing a secret passage that many wolves rush down. Warriors guide the pack down carefully, mothers carrying pups and holding onto the hands of their older children. Chris and Jack stay next to me with Eeva and her boys behind us. I could feel the tension in the air as we are led into a large room with couches and mattresses scattered around. Everyone finds a place to sit comfortably, my family and friends taking two large mattresses and pressing them together to huddle on. Finally, the last she-wolf with a small toddler in her arms enters the large room with the last of the Warriors filing in. The Warriors shut the large doors that can only be opened from inside this room. We were trapped.

"Everything will be fine. We will all be safe, so please stay calm." Eeva states from our spot in the farthest corner of the room. The wolves who were either family or close with one another from small groups and converse. A bassinet is placed beside me, courtesy of one of the Warriors, and I thank him, placing Julia inside and wrapping a warm blanket around her. I feel a blanket being draped over my shoulders as Eeva smiles at me.

"It can get cold in here. Tate will kill me if you get sick." She jokes, nudging my shoulders as her boys go off to find their friends.

"Thank you," I whisper, leaning into my friend. The two of us talk for a bit, my tired body now alert and waiting for news on Tate and the warriors.

"Luna?" I look up to see a group of pups walking over tentatively - their wide eyes staring at me with hopeful gazes. I quickly mask my emotions, putting on a brave face in front of these pups. It would be bad to show my own fear during my first crisis as Luna.

"Yes?" I ask with a friendly smile, feeling Eeva squeeze my hand reassuringly.

"Will you tell us a story?" A little girl about ten years old asks, and I smile a little more genuinely.

"Of course, that's not a problem. How about I tell you a legend my own mother taught me?" They all jump with excitement before taking a seat in front of me. More blankets are passed around to the children as other young pups come to hear the story.

"Long ago, before werewolves and vampires lived, gods and goddesses ruled the earth. They walked like us, talked like us, and ruled the humans. Some could change into animals, some lived in the forest, and others held dark secrets. There was this one goddess who was called Luna Dea, the moon goddess." I paused as their eyes twinkle.

"Luna Dea was happy. She was one with wolves that walked with her. The people loved her, and the gods adored her, but she wanted something. She wanted a child. For years, she walked the earth, watching humans raise their young and wishing for her own, but she knew that she needed a soulmate. One day, she came across a house in the woods. A man was cutting down fallen logs with wolves by his side. She was intrigued, and for days she stayed by his side. Little did Luna Dea know that Sat Dei, the Sun God, had been following her, wishing that she knew just how much he loved her-"

"What a stalker." Jack cuts me off, and I glare at him, watching as Chris smacks him upside the head and causing everyone to laugh. I roll my eyes at my cousin-in-law, enjoying this relaxed moment before turning to look back at the kids.

"-But Luna Dea was already in love. Sat Dei had an idea, and he left to the heavens to find a gift that Luna Dea would love, but it took years. When he returned, he found Luna Dea in the human man's arms, her belly round with children that would come any day.

"Furious, Sat Dei attacked, turning his gift of the stars into silver. For fear of her soulmate, Luna Dea bit the human, transferring her wolf power to him, a future Alpha, while the silver was stabbed through her heart."

"This stopped Sat Dei in his tracks. He looked on in horror at what he had done to his true love, who was now in the arms of the human. She turned to the father of her children, begging him to cut them out before she died, and he did. As she laid with her three children in her arms, the first werewolves born, she turned to Sat Dei and said with conviction, 'Your Children will be slaves of the night, your beautiful Sun their curse, while mine will know the loving embrace of the Moon." With those last sounds of her soft voice, she turns to her love, her soulmate, and says, 'May our children find their true half and know a love as strong as ours.' And at the highest peak of the full moon, her soul became one with her place in the sky. Stricken with grief, Sat Dei went to the nearest village and found a woman. For nights, he used her until she stood her belly round with child."

"He was overjoyed, his memory of Luna Dea and her last words a haze."

"Soon, the day came when three children were placed in his arms, and with joy, he took them out to see his sun. But they screamed as their skin burned. Quickly, he rushes inside, holding his babies as their mother came to help, picking one up only to scream in pain as the infant bites into her, draining her of blood. Sat Dei didn't know what to do other than to lure young women to his house to feed his babies. They aged faster than usual, and as they reached a month old, they were already the height of a four-year-old and could venture out at night."

"On a full moon night, Sat Dei looked up at the starry sky to see the moon looking down. He cried. It was Luna Dea, and he remembered her last words, realizing his children were slaves to the sun because of his actions."

"Grief coming into his soul faster than the day he killed Luna Dea, he did something no one thought would happen. He took a branch with a sharp end from an oak tree and stabbed his arms, legs, and stomach. Drawn by the blood, his children rush over to where he lays bleeding in their small house, and they began feeding on their father's body. As the sun rose, he took his place in the sky, forever chasing after Luna Dea. Today, we call their Children werewolves and vampires. When Luna Dea was stabbed with silver, it caused our weakness to the substance, and when Sat Dei stabbed himself with wood, he caused vampires to be weak to wooden stakes." I finish the story explaining our origins. It is a historical tale I memorized that my mother would tell me on long cold nights in front of our fireplace. The children clap and thank me for taking the time to tell this story as the older ones process my words. I could see some inquisitive minds that stayed behind to ask me about the legend, and I answer as best as I could. Some mothers nod at me in respect, admiration in their eyes while they usher their pups to comfortable spots trying to get them to sleep.

It took a few minutes for the pups to fall asleep. The adults huddle together, too anxious to sleep. The thoughts of what is happening outside swirl inside my mind. *Is Tate safe?* I wonder, looking at Julia, who sleeps peacefully.

"What does Pine Paw want with us?"

"Why are they here?"

"Will our pack be alright?" The other wolves voice their questions, causing a small pit of guilt to seep into my heart. I knew why Pine Paw was here. I turn my head to see Jack looking at me, sending me a reassuring smile while Chris leans against him, eyes closed.

'Open the link for me and Chris.' Jack mouths, and I nod, letting my mind focus on the two men I trusted.

[Are you okay?] Jack asks as soon as our link is opened. I sigh and send a weary smile his way.

[No, I want this to be over, and I want Tate.] I could feel tears forming in my eyes, and I shake my head. I couldn't cry right now when these wolves rely on me as their Luna to be strong for them.

[The only explanation is that they want you and Julia, Ross must have told them.] Chris speculates. I felt that something was off the moment Ross left the table when the Elders came to my house. It made sense that Pinepaw would attack now, but it is a suicide mission doing so. Bloodsvain is feared by many packs in the country.

[Get some rest. If something happens, we will wake you.] Jack suggests, pulling Chris closer to him. I know he is right and that I need sleep, but as I lay down, sleep decides to evade me as worry gnaws at my mind. I just hoped that Tate would be safe.

CHAPTER 17

"The poor Luna. Not even fully mated yet, and the Alpha is already on his death bed." A voice says loudly as growls sound afterwards with these disrespectful words.

"Shut up! What if she hears you? Besides, Doctor Rex said there is a chance he will survive." I jolt awake from these words, my eyes scanning for the source when I spot two she-wolves huddled together, their eyes darting about. I don't see any sympathy for the situation, and irritation floods me. It is wolves like these that cause disharmony in the pack.

Getting up and slowly walking towards the girls. I feel the others' eyes on me who wait for a good show even though the door to the shelter is open, and we may leave. Standing behind the two she-wolves, I let out a warning growl and watch as they stand straighter, fear coursing through them.

"I suggest you both shut up. Talking about your leaders behind their back, especially with one of them in the room, is grounds for punishment." I grind out, letting the power of a Luna suppress them. I let the two girls sweat for a moment as they realize their mistake before turning on my heels and walking away, letting the pressure ease off the two while taking a peek at my daughter, who is being fed by Chris.

"Your parents would be proud of you, Luna." Chris grins, using my new title. I roll my eyes at my cousin before a frown takes over. Where those girls speaking the truth, and is Tate injured? As if answering my question, a familiar face in the crowd makes their way out of the shelter. Mike approaches me, and it is then that I realize Eeva and her boys are gone.

"Laina, Doc told me to come to get you." His face holds a grim look, one that holds sympathy that is directed at me. I feel my heart drop as dread fills me. *Tate is okay, right?* Taking a shaky breath, Chris hands me Julia as Jack comes to stand behind me, giving me a shaky smile.

"Okay, Mike. Lead the way." I motion towards the door, letting my Head Warrior guide me towards the exit as we climb the stairs and exit the pantry. Chris and Jack stay behind me, making sure no wolf can rush ahead of me. I could tell what Mike and Doctor Rex have to say is serious.

Instead of taking me to the front door to drive to the hospital, I am lead to another room - one that is guarded heavily. I notice the elevator first, Mike pressing a button that allows our group entry as it ascends. Time feels like it is ticking by slowly, growing my anxiety. The elevator holds a sombre atmosphere as we pass each floor until landing on the fifth floor. Rushing out as soon as the elevators open, Mike leads us to a set of closed doors, his hands shaking as he opens the door. What greets me first is that annoying sound of beeping from the heart monitor. This sound causes my heart to stop momentarily as the scent of blood, and of my mate, reaches my nose.

"Laina." Eeva's strained voice reaches when I slowly pad into the room, taking note of the sterile environment. I turn my head to see my sister-in-law walk towards me, a strained smile on her face.

"We won and drove them away with no deaths, but-" Her voice cracks as she falls to the ground, hugging herself. I stand there, tears falling down my face as someone takes Julia out of my arms. I notice Jack giving me a sad smile as he adjusts Julia in his arms.

"Go to him, Laina. Chris and I can take care of Julia." Jack's voice reaches me as he steps away. I give a slight nod, turning to look at the figure on the bed, barely breathing, where the sound of the heart monitor beeps away. I hated that noise from my own time in the pack hospital, but right now, I was grateful for this annoyance. It meant that Tate is still alive. Taking a few hesitant steps before rushing to the side of the bed, I collapse beside Tate, clutching at the blankets that cover him.

"You...can't...leave...me!" I cry out, hiccupping between each word.

"Please...Tate, wake up." I plead, burying my face into his side and crying harder. I had already lost a child; I couldn't lose my mate as well. I cried like I did at Kelly's funeral, praying that the Moon Goddess will not take him away from me. Julia needed her father, and I needed my mate as well.

...

Beep

That sound is starting to get on my nerves, but it means that he is still alive. Tate is alive. I still have hope to hang on to.
Beep

"Hi, Tate. The Elders and I postponed the attack on Pine Paw until you wake up." I say, my words sounding hoarse. Slowly, I put Julia on his stomach, watching her move slightly towards his face. It's been two weeks since Tate went into a coma. I refused to return home without him, and a room next door was set up for Julia and me to live in while we wait for Tate to wake up.

"Julia is getting bigger. She misses her Daddy." This time my voice is a whisper, and I carefully move Julia so that she is by his side, moving his arm so that it wraps around her. I hated knowing his life still hung in the unknown.

"Please, Tate, it's been two weeks. We need you." I cry out, my head lowering to the bed as tears flow again for the umpteenth time. I don't know how long I sat in this position, my body shaking from my sobs. I needed Tate more than ever to open his eyes.

"Laina?" I straighten in my seat and turn to see Doctor Rex standing at the door. His face is grim as his lips are set in a firm line.

"What is it?" I ask, trying to sound strong, although my tear-stained face says otherwise.

"We need to talk. It has been two weeks, and he is still on life support. The coma he is in is getting worse." More tears flow, and I try to wipe them away as quickly as I can, but I couldn't help it, and in seconds, I felt Rex wrapping his arms around me and letting me cry. Finally, my sobs came to an end, and Rex hands me a handkerchief to wipe my tears.

"I'm glad someone can sleep through this." He states, and I turn to find Julia snuggled up to the man who stepped up to be her father. He will forever be her father in our eyes.

"Just continue, please," I whisper, and I hear Rex sigh. I hated long-winded stories, and Rex learned to get right to the point with me.

"We need an answer by next week, but wolves can't survive on life support forever. And his time is almost up. I'm sorry you have to go through this, but as his mate you decide whether to take him off of it or not." I could feel his eyes on me, and I just nod. Finally, the door clicked shut and I am left alone with my mate and our daughter. His life is in my hands now, and only I could decide if he will stay on life support or if I let him go and join the other side with Kelly and our loved ones.

CHAPTER 18

Beep

"Are you sure, Laina?" The sound of the heart monitor's steady beeping follows Eeva's question as I look at Tate's still form.

Beep

The sound continues on as everyone looks at me with worry in their gaze.

"I'm sure. It's better than letting my mate suffer." I whisper out. Eeva nods, knowing that the decision for her younger brother to be taken off life support lies in my hand.

Beep

Rex slowly walks over to the life support machine and lets out a long, sad sigh. I could see the pain in his eyes as he stares at Tate with a sad smile.

"Goodbye, friend." He says sadly before flicking the machine off. Slowly everything comes to a stop. The only thing working is the heart monitor for now. Eeva takes Julia from my arms and motions for me to go to Tate. With tears in my eyes, I stand at his bedside and take his hand in mine.

Beep

My heart breaks at his still form, and with one last try, I open the link just between us, bending down and kissing his lips gently.

[I love you.] I confess with tears flowing down my face and onto his as I stand straight. I wipe away the wetness on his cheeks as I try my best to give a wobbly smile. Just over a month with Tate and I knew that my life will never be the same without him.

The sound of the heart monitor slows down, with each beep taking longer to sound. My heart cracks just a bit. It takes everything in me not to break down now.

Beep

The final beep sounds, and the room goes silent. With tears streaming down my face once more and sobs ready to wrack my body, I turn away from the bed, ready to walk away.

BEEP

BEEP

BEEP

BEEP

My steps falter briefly. The machine is going off, and I turn with wide-eyed at the heart monitor that made a comeback stronger than I thought it ever would. That annoying sound is something I relish with joy as it can only mean one thing.

[La....] it was weak, but I knew it was Tate.

[I'm here, baby, please wake up.] I link him, rushing to his side and clasping his hand.

[Laina....] His voice is louder, and my tears turn from ones of pain to ones of joy.

"Whatever you did, Luna, it worked. He is waking up." Mike's mate, Ashlyn, a nurse assigned to help take care of Tate, says from the door. No one else dares to come near as I clutched his hand tighter.

[Laina, where...] I hear his question loud and clear even if he can't finish it.

[I'm here. All you need to do is wake up.] I reply as I looked to the sky outside the big window, staring at the moon that shines down on us.

[Just open your eyes] I plead, turning my head to find myself staring into forest green eyes.

"I...did." His voice is hoarse, and I couldn't help but laugh as he states the obvious, letting go of his hand to fall into his chest and cry, clutching his shirt. I feel a warm hand pet my head as fingers run through my hair gently, and I look to see that it is Tate doing this with what little strength he has, his face looking guilty.

"Sorry...you...waited," Tate whispers, and I laugh again.

"I'll always wait for you baby, I love you," I reply before moving to kiss all over his face, ending at his lips. His lips move with mine in a heated, passion-filled kiss, feeling his hand clutch my hair.

"Um, can you guys save that until after he gets better and you are in your own home?" Eeva says awkwardly, coming to stand with Julia in her arms. I pull away from Tate with a blushing face forgetting that others were standing with us when joy overcame me when Tate awakened.

"Can....I?" He looks at our daughter, and I smile, taking her from Eeva and putting her beside him with his arm around our little girl. His face is one of joy as he snuggles our baby close to him, relief filling me.

Thank you Goddess. I pray, closing my eyes. Everyone stays for a few more minutes before Rex, with tears in his eyes, orders them to leave before having a bassinet and other baby equipment rolled into the room for Julia. I refused to leave Tate's side now that he is awake. With everyone gone and Julia asleep, I let Tate snuggle into me, his head on the crook of my neck with arms wrapped tightly around me. My hands play with his hair gently, feeling his body relax as his eyes droop with exhaustion.

"I love you." He whispers, and I kiss his cheek.

"I love you too," I reply back, smiling when he falls asleep with a happy grin on his face. I stay awake a little longer watching the man I love. He did everything he could to protect Julia and I when Pinepaw attacked, and I had almost lost him. I am just happy I have a second chance. Yawning, I snuggle closer to Tate, hugging his body to mine as tightly as I can without hurting him.

"Get better soon, my love," I whisper before falling asleep.

CHAPTER 19

"Laina, I am fine!" Tate sighs as I fluff his pillow for the umpteenth time today. I couldn't help but hover over my mate the way he did with me when I first woke from my emergency surgery.

"No, you're not, so stop complaining and let me pamper you," I argue back, hearing Tate mutter something about me being a worrywart. How the tides have turned. It's been three days since Tate first woke up from his coma. I spent most days either curled up in bed with Tate and Julia watching T.V. The only times I leave this room are to use the washroom and take Julia outside to get some fresh air.

When Tate is asleep, I find myself at the desk Loren and Mike brought in, going over pack paperwork with the two men and Eeva's help. Rex would come in every now and then to check on Tate's condition, then would leave Tate, Julia, and me for the rest of the night. Deciding that Tate is thoroughly tucked in and comfortable, I stretch for a moment, ready to go to the desk to get some work done.

"If you want to pamper me, there is a great way that I can think of," Tate says, catching me off guard as he grasps my wrist and pulls me on top of his body. I feel him wince when my knee hits the wound on his thigh, and I try my best to get free and off of him, only to be held tighter by my mate.

"Cuddle with me, please. We haven't spent much time alone, and I just want to feel you close." His voice is a low, hoarse whisper sending shivers down my spine. I relent to his request and rest my head on his shoulder, snuggling in close. The room is silent as his hands slowly moved from my back, under my shirt and ran up and down my sides, slow and gentle, sending tingles of pleasure through me where his hands touch my skin. I sigh in contentment, gently kissing Tate's jawline.

"I love you, Laina." He whispers, turning his head to kiss my forehead.

"I love you too Tate," I whisper back, moving my head and connecting our lips together. His hands stop moving, pulling me impossibly closer to his body. My hands snake up his chest and around his neck, bringing his head closer to mine as our kiss deepens. I squeak in surprise when Tate manages to flip us so that my back is pressed against the bed and Tate on top. My legs wrap around his waist and moan as our lips continue to collide with our passionate kiss. Tate slowly grinds against me, sending more pleasure travelling inside me, causing me to gasp. Tate takes this opportunity to plunge his tongue into my mouth as one hand slowly explores along my stomach to rest on my breast. Another moan escapes my lips, and I flick my tongue across his, gaining a feral moan from him as he presses his bulge against me, and I curse the jeans I decided to wear today. Slowly we pull apart, panting from the kiss. His eyes were dark and filled with lust, and I had a feeling my eyes matched his as he leans his forehead on mine and takes a deep breath.

"God, you're so beautiful." He groans out before claiming my mouth in another passionate kiss, one arm supporting him above me, while his free hand explores under my shirt, my own hands feeling every muscle, every scar and every movement of his body. I wanted him. I wanted him above me, below me and inside me. I wanted to completely mate with him. The kiss ends prematurely as the door opens, causing both of us to growl and glare at the intruder.

"Hey, this is a room for patients. If the two of you want to make love, then go home, for crying out loud!" Rex exclaims, holding his hands up in surrender and rolling his eyes. It took a while for my hormones to settle down before Rex's words settle in, and happiness fills me.

"Wait, I can go home?" Tate asks with hope lacing his voice. I smile and push Tate off of me gently, making him sit on the bed. I push myself up to sit cross-legged on the bed, my hand reaching out to hold onto Tate's.

"Yes, you've healed nicely over the last few days, and your scans show that your brain is functioning normally," Rex answers, chuckling at Tate's enthusiasm.

"Just take it easy at home and rest, and no rough sex. I get you two haven't completed the mating process yet, but I don't need to see any of you as a patient again for a while." I blush as Rex continues his instructions of what Tate needs to do when we return home. Part of me understands that he still needed time to rest, but another part wanted to fully be mated to him as quick as possible. Rex stays for a moment to do a quick check-up on Tate before allowing Ashlyn to come in and remove the I.V. from his arm. After getting the final go-ahead to leave, Rex and his team remove the medical equipment to be stored away in the pack house for emergency use leaving Tate and I alone.

"Now, where were we?" He asks, his voice husky as he leans his head towards mine and kisses me passionately once again.

"How about we go home first, go for a relaxing bath-" I start to say the moment we pull away to catch our breath.

"And continue where we left off before being so rudely interrupted." Tate finishes my sentence twirling a lock of my air around his fingers. I smile and nod, climbing off the bed and holding my hand out for Tate to take. I watch my mate slowly stand to his feet, wincing from the almost healed injuries before taking my hand and pulling me in for a hug.

"I'm driving," I say sternly, looking up to catch Tate's

frown at me.

"No, I am." He counters, rolling his eyes at me. I couldn't help but sigh in exasperation and push him playfully onto the bed again while taking the keys to the jeep out of my pocket.

"You are in no shape to drive, so I will. No arguments." I rebut with, watching him slowly stand and try to take the keys from me, growling when I jump back out of his reach. For a few minutes, he tries to take the keys away, and I focus on staying just out of his reach.

"Fine, you can drive." He relents frowning at me and pouting like a child. I chuckle at his behaviour and make my way into his arms, standing on my toes to plant a kiss on his cheek. From there, I take his hand and the two of us walk into the hallway and take the elevator down to the main floor. On our way out of the pack house, the two of us pass by pack members that congratulate Tate on getting better. I felt like a huge weight has been lifted off the pack now that their Alpha is better.

After chatting with a few of the wolves, Tate and I manage to finally find solace in the Jeep. I catch Tate sighing, taking a deep breath of air that doesn't smell like the pack hospital and reach out to squeeze his hand. No more hospital trips for us for a while.

Turning the Jeep on, I put the Jeep into drive and head in the direction of home.

CHAPTER 20

Pulling into the driveway, I shut off the Jeep, silence filling the interior. It felt good being home after spending over two weeks at the pack house, and Eeva promised to take care of Julia for tonight at her house. I think Eeva is secretly happy to have a little girl over for the night as she has told me many times she is trying to have a daughter with Loren. A soft snore beside me catches my attention. When I turn to look at Tate, I giggle, a soft smile on my face, as I watch my mate doze off, head back against the seat. He looks so peaceful with the fall light streaming in through the window.

Slowly, I lean over, making sure not to wake Tate, and place a gentle kiss on his lips. I lean back, ready to pull away until strong hands pull me close, and I find my chest pressed against Tate's. Warm lips press against mine as we move in a slow rhythm. I let out a small moan when he nips at my bottom lip before his tongue pries open my mouth and delves inside. Our tongues dance around for dominance until I give in, letting him take control of our kiss and relish in the pleasure he brings forth in me. His hands snake around to my ass, groping me and somehow bringing me onto his lap to straddle him where I feel his large bulge press against my sensitive area.

Slowly I grind against his bulge, causing not only a moan to escape my lips but a feral groan from him. His hands guide my hips down onto the bulge and move in a way that causes enough friction to have me pull away from the kiss and cry out in pleasure. Both of us are gasping for breath and eyes glazed with raw pleasure.

"Bedroom, now!" Tate orders in a husky growl, his voice barely a whisper as his lips attack the sensitive part of my neck that has me wet and needy. I am too horny to argue with Tate about his possessive attitude. I wanted – no – needed him badly. I needed to feel his body pressed into mine with how I craved his touch. Needing the release only Tate could bring me to.

Leaving my neck to kiss me once more, Tate pulls away to rest his forehead on mine, needing to catch his breath. I smile lustfully at him, my own lips moving to attack his neck and leaving hickeys in my wake and getting a lust-filled growl out of Tate. Opening the passenger door, I slowly climb out, releasing my assault on his neck, ready to move to unlock the front door, only to find myself pressed against the Jeep with every inch of Tate pressed against me. His hard bulge presses against my stomach while he caresses my exposed skin. I shiver from both the pleasure caused by Tate groping my sensitive breasts ad the cold air letting out another loud moan.

"Let's go inside, Laina." He says against my mouth, then continuing the deep kiss and forcing me to walk backwards to the front door, pulling away long enough to unlock and open it. Once inside, the door is slammed shut and fingers pinch and pull at my nipples, eliciting loud moans from my mouth that get swallowed by Tate's kisses. A hand leaves its assault on my breasts to weave its way into my hair, pulling my head back as Tate bites and sucks on my skin.

"I want you, Laina. I want you underneath me as I make love to you." Tate groans against the base of my neck.

"Then take me." I consent, giving a soft smile as an astonished look fills Tate's eyes. I squeal in surprise when his hands leave my body, only to lift me bridal style into his arms, causing me to worry about his remaining injuries.

"Be careful, baby!" I exclaim with concern, placing my hand against his cheek gently and looking at his body, checking to see if his wounds were aggravated.

"I'm fine. The only medicine I need is you." He retorts with rolling his eyes and silencing any protest I have with yet another passionate kiss, his tongue forcing its way into my mouth once again. Distracted by my mate, I find myself being lowered onto our bed with Tate between my legs. He slowly grinds into me, and I meet his movements with my own as our hands slowly undress each other. Hovering above me, Tate's eyes take in my naked body, his right hand caressing my cheek, and I turn my face to kiss his palm.

"You're so beautiful." He whispers, his eyes unable to hide the love he has for me behind the gloss of lust. I blush at his words, looking away, knowing I still had a small amount of pregnancy weight and scars from the surgery on me still not fully healed. For the first time, I feel a slight bubble of insecurity rise inside me.

"What's the matter?" Tate asks, tilting my head so that I am once again looking at him.

"I'm not beautiful," I whisper, and he smiles.

"You're right. You're gorgeous, smart, strong, and brave. Most of all, you're mine, and I love you." My heart flutters. In Tate's eyes, I am perfect, and I feel his love pour through our bond. Wrapping my arms around his shoulders, I pull Tate forward and kiss him passionately, tears of happiness pooling in my eyes.

"I love you too," I whisper, pulling away to catch my breath, getting the most dazzling and affectionate smile from my loving mate.

"I want to do this right, Laina. I want to make love to you slowly when I make you mine forever." Tate says, running the hand that caresses my face down my chin, over my breast and past my stomach to come between my legs and tease the wet folds of my entrance. I gasp when he slips a finger inside me, moving gently against my wet walls and causing me to cry out. He doesn't stop there when his lips descend onto one of my nipples, and his free hand pulls at the other one making me into nothing but a moaning, lustful mess.

"Does it feel good?" He asks, adding another finger inside me as I clench at his arm, shouting his name while an orgasm causes my body to twitch with extreme pleasure.

"I'll take that as a yes." He whispers, bringing his lips to mine and kissing me, my lips opening to allow his tongue inside. His fingers slowly stop moving inside me while his lips move down my body past my stomach until I feel his breath at my entrance. His warm tongue sweeps across my clitoris, licking up my juices from my orgasm, causing another gasp to exit my lips. One hand clutches at his hair and the other the bedsheets while he licks and nips at my soaking wet vagina. As I reach my second climax, Tate pulls away before I could orgasm, causing a noise of protest to leave my mouth. He kisses his way back up my body until his lips wet with my juices press against my own in a heated kiss. Spreading my legs further, he positions his hard cock against my opening, rubbing the tip against me, making me move my hips in hopes of gaining release.

"You okay, Laina?" Tate asks with a smirk, one hand pressing against my stomach to stop me from moving.

"No, I want more." I whimper, pressing against the tip of his throbbing rod and moaning from the pleasure it brought, hearing him groan.

"Okay, but I am going slow." He groans out as I move against him again, wrapping my legs around his waist. His hands stop my movement once more, and he holds me in place, leaning forward and kissing me deeply as he moves. His tip enters me inch by inch, my wet walls helping him move smoothly until I felt his body pressed firmly against mine and his length was buried deep inside. Pausing inside me, Tate's body shivers with the pleasure of us beginning the mating process. His lips move from mine to nip at the skin on my neck as he begins to thrust in and out. Each thrust squelches from the juices that accumulate inside me. I cry out in pleasure and scream Tate's name, moving my hips in sync with his. His thrusts increase in speed, with our bodies sweaty from exertion, until the pleasure builds inside me. My eyes glaze over for a moment with lust as I call out to Tate, feeling his canines extend. With a final thrust, I find my release, my juices coating Tate's and my thighs when he releases his hot seed inside me. His canines pierce my skin, marking me as his, as my lips find the crook of his neck, my own canines piercing him.

Tate and I were finally fully mated.

Our canines retract when the pleasure subsides, and we catch our breaths. Tate leans his forehead against mine, grinning like a child in a candy store as he looks into my eyes.

"I love you, beautiful," he says, nuzzling our noses together.

"And I love you, sexy," I whisper, giggling as he nuzzles my cheek. I feel him slowly pull out, and I couldn't help but moan slightly with how sensitive I am feeling his body shake with his chuckles.

"Are you up for round two?" He asks, and I quickly shake my head no, yawning.

"Can we just snuggle and fall asleep?" I ask, my body feeling drained of energy. Tate chuckles again, flopping onto his side of the bed and reaching out to pull me to his side. The blanket is wrapped around us as I snuggle closer to him, a content smile on my face.

"Sleep then. I will be here with you, my beautiful little mate." I yawn at Tate's words and smile, resting my head on his warm shoulder and drift off to sleep.

CHAPTER 21

I groan slightly as the warm body underneath me moves. My eyes slowly open to see the soft morning light illuminating my mate beside me as his soft lips press against my temple. My body felt sore, and a slight tinge of pain in my neck brought back the memories of last night. Tate and I have mated and marked each other.

A grin spreads across my face as I nuzzle against Tate's neck, catching sight of the mark I left on him. I felt whole, with Tate being completely mine and me being completely his.

"Good morning, beautiful," Tate whispers, his hand running through my hair gently. I close my eyes, relishing in his pampering, letting out a yawn.

"Good morning, baby," I reply, my voice laced with sleep. For a few minutes, we just lay in bed enjoying each other's silent company and taking in the first morning as a mated pair. I missed lying in our bed together away from the sounds of a hospital room, and being home alone with Tate felt perfect. Being home felt like the best place to be with no one to bother us, and no nurses to walk in and disturb our rest every so often throughout the day. It's a play I felt safe and secured in with Tate beside me.

"Hey, Laina." Tate whispers, his fingers drawing slow circles on my shoulder.

"Yes, baby?" I ask, tilting my head to look into his dark green eyes. I love his eyes.

"When was the last time you shifted?" I could hear the

concern in his voice. Wolves have an urge to shift and release their primal side; it keeps us healthy and sane. The only exception for this is if we are pregnant or seriously wounded.

"Two weeks after I found out I was pregnant. Sam and his Warriors were hunting me down, and if I hadn't shifted, I would have been caught." I answer honestly. I remember how terrified I felt that day. I had found a nice town to hide in, renting out a small one-bedroom cottage while I figured out what to do. After a couple of days of feeling safe away from Pine Paw, Sam and his Warriors barged into town looking for me. My landlady called the cottage phone and informed me about these men looking for me, and the best excuse I could give to the nice elderly human is that he was an abusive ex trying to drag me back home. She bought me some time to pack and leave. That day, I shifted once again and ran for my life, with only my bags on me. I decided to stay in wolf form for a week until I made good time and was days away from Sam. It took a while for the Pine Paw wolves to find me after that, and I took off once again to find myself in Bloods-vain territory.

"If Rex gave you the okay to shift, we could go outside in the backyard, and you can let loose," Tate suggests, and I grin. This would be the first time my mate would see my wolf form, and I can't wait to show him. Bouncing off the bed, I rush into the closet, hearing Tate chuckle behind me and take one of his shirts that covers me like a short dress and bring a set of clothes to my mate.

"Excited to shift?" Tate asks to laugh as I help him dress into a pair of baggy track pants and a V-neck t-shirt. I could see the extent of his still-healing wounds, and my heart clenches. I knew last night took a toll on his body, but the need to mate with each other and be together forever was intense and took hold of us. I'm proud our primal instincts took over but made a small vow to not do anything else until Tate is healed completely.

"Yes, I miss running so much and really need to stretch

my legs, especially in wolf form," I answer as Tate stands. He takes my hand, and the two of us make our way slowly down the stairs and into the kitchen, where we slip out the back door. Tate takes a seat on one of the padded lounge chairs, and I run inside to grab a blanket to wrap around him. Once I am satisfied that Tate is warm and comfortable, I quickly remove the shirt from my body, hearing a lustful growl from my mate and the heat of his gaze skimming down my back and ass, causing a blush to crawl on my cheeks. With a leap off the deck, I shift in midair, landing gracefully on my paws and shaking out my fur. Stretching my limbs, I turn my blue-white fur with black-tipped paws body to look at Tate, his eyes in awe.

"You're a beautiful wolf," Tate whispers while I pad up the deck stairs to come site beside him, my tail thumping against the deck happily. His hand reaches out to run his fingers through my fur, and I let out a soft whisper of pleasure, closing my eyes happily.

"Why don't you run for a bit around the area? I'll be fine." My ears perk up with this suggestion, and I look to Tate with a wolfish grin.

[You sure, baby?] I ask uncertainly into our link. Part of me wanted to stay close to Tate, but another part of me needed a good run.

"Positive. Link me where you are ever so often." Tate assures, poking my nose playfully. I lick his fingertips before taking off. My paws carry me through the forest around our house first, leading me to the lake with the floating gazebo, where I take a drink of the crisp and clean-tasting water. My eyes scan the area, watching ducks and geese swim across the crystal-clear water, and I think about how good their tender flesh would feel between my canines before taking off again. I explore as far as I feel comfortable with, linking Tate every now and then of the areas I pass and which pack members I cross paths with. The wind rushes through my fur, and the scents of our territory bring a sense of belonging through me, causing my heart to swell with pride and happiness. Each pine tree holds a unique scent that brings a touch of never-ending life, while the oak, maple, and birch trees slowly have their leaves falling and decaying onto the cold forest floor below. Another hour passes by while I push my body as far as I can, leaping over fallen logs and splashing through puddles and small streams, but I know I have to head back soon. With a sigh, I loop back towards home. Two hours have passed with the run in wolf form, leaving me feeling refreshed and renewed with all that has weighed my mind and body down the last few weeks. Taking a shortcut Tate and I would normally take on our walks, I reach home in about thirty minutes, seeing Tate with his phone out just in time to snap a picture of me.

"Did you enjoy yourself?" Tate asks as I shift and put the large shirt back on, crawling into his lap to snuggle with him on the lounge chair.

"Yes. When you're better, let's go for a run together." I reply, kissing his jaw and resting my head on his shoulder.

"Sounds like a plan. Eeva texted me just a few minutes ago. She is bringing Julia home and should be here soon." I groan slightly at this information. Part of me is enjoying have Tate to myself, and I didn't want anyone coming over today. But I missed my pup too much and wanted Julia home.

"Does this mean our quiet time is over?" I ask, getting a chuckle from my mate. He tilts my head back gently to plant a long kiss on my lips, pulling away with a smirk and leaving me breathless after a few minutes.

"We can have quiet time to ourselves later tonight, so don't worry." He promises a blush on my cheeks once again. I had a feeling it would be hard to not make love to my mate so that he can heal properly over these next few days. With a sigh, I climb off Tate and stretch before helping Tate to his feet.

We walk into the house. Tate goes to sit in the living room, and I make my way upstairs to put on a pair of thongs and leggings, keeping Tate's shirt on because I just wanted to lounge around the house today. Heading back downstairs, I catch Tate holding the front door open while Eeva pushes a stroller inside.

"Hey, Eev-" I start to greet my sister-in-law and friend.

"Shh, my niece is sleeping." Eeva scolds, parking the stroller beside the bench in our entranceway to take off her shoes. I roll my eyes at her and quietly walk over to peer inside to see the angelic face of Julia deep in her sleep. I missed my little girl so much and couldn't help but run a finger gently across her chubby cheeks.

"I'll bring her to her room," Tate whispers as I straighten up, letting him pull the stroller closer to where he stands. Carefully he bends down to unstrap Julia from her stroller and cradle her in his arms. It felt great seeing him hold our pup outside of the patient room in the pack house.

"Do you need help?" I ask, stepping closer to plant a soft kiss on Julia's forehead and getting ready to assist Tate up the stairs.

"No, I'll just take my time." He reassures his eyes, focused on the sleeping baby in his arms. A soft smile plays on my lips, and I step back to give Tate room to turn around.

"Okay then. Call out if you need help." I agree. He smiles at me and kisses my forehead before making his way upstairs. I knew better than to wait for him and hurt his alpha pride, so I turn to Eeva, who has a smile on her lips and a knowing glint in her eyes.

"So, how does it feel to be completely his?" I blush at her words, my face a heated crimson.

"I don't know what you mean?" I feign ignorance and turn, heading towards the kitchen with my growling stomach protest because of the lack of food.

"Please, I can smell my brother all over you and inside you. Plus, the house reeks of like, did you guys do it in the hallway or something?" I feel my cheeks heat up even more as I busy myself with turning on the oven, grabbing a box of Delissio frozen pizza from the fridge and popping the pepperoni party size into the hot oven. I just ignore my friend and turn on the kettle to make some tea to sip on.

"C'mon, I know you're fully mated to him now. I can see the mark peeking out from under the collar of that shirt you're wearing." I didn't know how red my face is, but I smile, my hand reaching for the sensitive spot on my neck. I turn to face my friend, finally conceding to spill the details.

"It feels amazing, and it was amazing, and Eeva, I can't wait to fee-"

"Okay, too many details." I laugh at her reaction, a look of horror on her face as I was about to spill all the details of how amazing sex with Tate was last night.

"Well, you asked." I come back with, smirking at the look of horror still plastered on her face.

"But, that's my brother!" She practically yells, running her hand through her hair.

"You still asked." I shrug, pouring a cup of tea for us. She sighs in defeat and sits down at the table, and after checking the pizza, I join her, bringing the mugs over.

"So, when do you want to go shopping for some new clothes?" I laugh at the random question, at Eeva's attempt to change the subject when the sounds of the front door opening and closing reach us. Seconds later, Chris and Jack walk into the kitchen carrying take-out boxes.

"Oh, you're up. We went and got some take-out, but I smell pizza." I laugh at Jack's words and watch as he and Chris set the food on the table. I couldn't help but take a whiff of the Chinese food wafting from the containers, my stomach growling for food as soon as possible.

"By the way, Laina, was that your wolf I saw earlier today?" Chris asks, going to the cupboard to grab some plates. I smile happily, making my way to check on the pizza and nod.

"Yep, I needed a good run and haven't shifted in months. I needed to let loose." I respond. The smell of the pepperoni pizza spills out into the kitchen with the golden crust signalling it being cooked. Taking the pizza out of the oven, I rummage through a drawer for a pizza cutter coming out victorious. While I cut the pizza, Chris and Jack set the table. The sounds of footsteps on the stairs signal Tate joining us, and just as I put the pizza on the table with the Chinese food. I smile when Tate and I take the bench sitting across from Chris and Jack with Eeva at the end of the table.

"This is what I needed. My family and some take-out." Tate exclaims as he squeezes me closely, planting a kiss on the top of my head and everyone else chuckling. It's been a hectic month since Tate and I first met and just being able to appreciate the small things together made the things we went through worth it.

"So Eeva, where are the rugrats and your mate at today?" Chris asks, piling Chinese food onto his plate. I quickly snatch the spring rolls just in time to place a couple onto Tate and my plates before passing the appetizer around. Jack has a habit of eating all the spring rolls, which Chris and I hated.

"They went to the cabin about two hours away from here with their dad for the weekend. They want to soak up the last few rays of sun before snow kicks in so I have the house to myself." Eeva answers happily, stuffing a slice of pizza into her mouth. I smile at the normality, filling mine and Tate's plate and enjoying this night. The five of us talk for a while, Chris disappearing once to get a crying Julia, cradled in her father's arms as Tate feeds her. Sometime around seven, Eeva left, wanting to enjoy the alone time she rarely has. I couldn't help but laugh at her enthusiasm as she talks about the things she is going to do without having to deal with children. After Eeva left, Jack and Chris went to bed. They have been slowly renovating a house they found and had slept at the pack house last night to give Tate and me some privacy. I couldn't wait for the two of them to move out.

With a quiet house and Julia once again in her room asleep for the night, Tate and I find ourselves snuggling in front of the fireplace. His hands draw shapes on my back as we lay on the sofa held in each other's embrace.

"Have I ever told you how much you mean to me?" Tate asks quietly, turning my head so that we are looking into each other's eyes.

"Yes, whenever you get the chance to, you tell me," I answer, my voice barely above a whisper.

"Well, I don't say it enough." He adds, bending his head forward and gently kissing me. My hands cling to his shirt as our lips move in sync slowly, a small moan leaving my lips when he flips us over so that Tate lies on top of me. Pulling away breathless, he kisses the tip of my nose before resting his forehead on top of mine.

"Laina, you are the most beautiful, talented, amazing person I have ever known. You are my queen, my best friend and my true love, and I will always be here for you. If I make you mad, I will fight for you to smile and love me again. You make me happy, and you bring the sunshine back into my life." He smiles shyly at me before he kisses my lips once again - his lips and my own moving slightly more urgently. The kiss ends too soon, and we pull away panting slightly, our foreheads pressed together once again and tears well in my eyes.

"Why are you crying? Are you hurt?" I can feel Tate tense above me, his face filled with worry and his eyes scanning for any signs of injury. I giggle at his reaction and wrap my arms around his next, pulling Tate closer to me and burying my face into the crook of his neck.

"They're happy tears." I giggle, kissing his mark gently. Tate sighs with relief, turning us until I am lying on top of him again. His fingers wrap around my hair, playing with the chestnut locks staring into my eyes.

"I love you, Tate. I love you so much it hurts when I am not with you." I whisper, feeling the tears of joy slip down my cheeks. Tate gently moves so that the two of us are sitting, his arms wrapped around me, keeping me on his lap and hugging me tightly to his body.

"And I love you, Laina. You're my world, and I will do everything I can to protect you." He whispers, nuzzling my own mark that he left on me last night. One I will have for the rest of my life. I nod against his shoulder with his words, pulling back from the hug just to kiss him passionately, feeling his arms hold me tighter against him. His hands move to my hips, and he lifts me up as he stands, my legs wrapping around his waist, and his noticeable erection pressed to my thigh as he carries me to the direction of the stairs and up to our bedroom.

Passion ignites within us, my body sizzling with the pleasure of every touch. His lips find every sensitive area, sucking and kissing the skin, causing a flood of wetness to form between my legs. Our clothes are torn off in haste, the two of us just wanting to be close with only skin touching and no barriers to come between us until his length is nestled deep inside me.

We spend the night lost in each other's touch, crying with pleasure, with each release giving a silent vow to always protect and love each other as our primal urges take over.

CHAPTER 22

I groan at the bright room, burying my head under one of the large pillows. My body felt sore from the events of the last two nights, causing me to wonder if Tate is fully healed or not. No man should be this energetic when on bed rest. As my consciousness settles in, I realize that I am pressed under Tate, his hand removing the pillow from my head and the feel of his hard length still inside me from how we passed out last night. The memories of last night flash through my head with each position my body bend to Tate's will, and I moan, my body becoming sensitive again

"Someone having issues?" Tate's husky voice fills my ears as he slowly moves inside me, massaging my sore, sensitive walls. I moan again, arching my back to feel even more, gaining a chuckle at my wanton reaction from my mate.

"I'll take this as a yes then, baby." He whispers, his lips finding my mark and nipping at the sensitive skin. He picks up speed, the sounds of moaning and grunting filling the early morning air.

...

I wake to the smell of food and lavender tea, my groggy eyes opening to see a tray set on my side of the table with a red tulip and a note. A gentle smile spreads across my face at the sight of Tate's handwriting and a shirt of his placed beside the tray. Sitting up in bed, I stretch my sore body, noticing the bruises and love bites from Tate. I chuckle at his possessiveness in always finding a way to leave marks on me and reach for the large shirt, tugging it on.

Tate walks in just as I reach for the tea with a squirming Julia in one arm and a bottle in his free hand. He settles in beside me on the bed as I eat, feeding Julia. I reach for my phone, taking a chance to snap a picture of my little family and catching Tate off guard. He informs me that Chris and Jack went to their house to continue their renovations, leaving the three of us home alone.

"So, I was thinking we could have a movie night," Tate says out of nowhere a smile on his face as he lays a fed and changed Julia on our bed between us.

"We can go to the mall, find some movies to watch and get some snacks to have a night in. I think your cousin and his mate will be staying in their house for the night since it's almost ready for them to move in." I smile at the suggestion, happy to know that Chris and Jack will be leaving our house. It makes having time alone with Tate easier with them gone.

"Okay, sounds like fun," I reply after thinking about it, finishing the last of my food. I place the tray onto the side table beside me and carefully move closer to Tate, wrapping my arms around him and nuzzling his neck. Part of me did not want to move from our comfortable bed, but the idea of a movie night date with my mate has the giddiness of my young age taking over me.

Deciding to get dressed, I leave Julia in Tate's care and quickly go for a shower, grabbing a light fall dress from the closet first to put on after cleaning my body from our earlier morning activity. Each step I take has me wincing slightly, and I catch Tate smirking at my discomfort. *Asshole.*

The running water eases the slight pain from my body, making moving and walking a lot easier by the time I turn off the shower and step out to get ready to leave. I towel dry my hair and body slipping into some lacey undergarments before pulling the dress on and piling my semi-damp hair into a messy bun on top of my head. Grabbing a pair of flats from the closet, I pick up my purse and Head downstairs, where I see Tate readying Julia for our excursion.

"Are you ready to go?" Tate asks, lifting the car seat into his arms as I grab the diaper bag.

"Yes, I am. No sex tonight, please. I need a break." I answer, stating my need to skip on our nightly – um - exercise. My mate smirks at me, planting a quick kiss on my lips and agreeing as we leave the house and into the jeep. He secures Julia's car seat in the back behind the driver's seat as I place the diaper bag on the floor in the back before we climb in and pull out of the driveway.

The drive to the mall is filled with us talking about our favourite childhood movies. Tate was shocked that I grew up seeing almost all Disney movies. I pointed out that with a gay cousin and his mate raising me, I was raised differently from other werewolves and would be subjected to romance movies and Disney marathons, and the motivational message of I can do anything if I just put my mind to it. They built my confidence and gave me the freedom to learn who I was and am growing up.

After pulling into the mall parking lot, the two of us make quick work of getting Julia's car seat connected to the stroller. With her safe and secured, Tate takes the lead in pushing the stroller into the mall entrance.

"So where to first?" I ask, hooking my arms around Tate's bicep, feeling him flex with my touch. I catch sight of people doing double-takes at us as we walk by and have to do my best to hold in my laughter. I guess seeing a six-foot-seven-inch man built like a bodybuilder pushing a baby-pink stroller and a short girlfriend beside him is a sight to see.

"We could head to Wal-Mart and look in the electronic section and grab snacks all in one go." He suggests, and I nod. Wal-Mart is located on the other side of the mall, and we took the time to window shop and enjoy the stroll. Before we reach

Wal-Mart, I come to a stop in front of Build-A-Bear, practically dragging Tate into the store to create three wolf stuffies for each of us. I could see his bemused look as I childishly run around searching for the right outfits to dress the wolf stuffie in clothes suited to Tate and my style finishing with a baby wolf that once paid for I place beside Julia in her car seat.

"Was that fun?" Tate asks, chuckling, the boxes housing each stuffed animal in the basket at the bottom of the stroller.

"Yes. I've always wanted to go there and do that as a child. Just never had the chance too, and now we each have a Build-A-Bear." I giggle out the answer, my eyes sparkling with joy. We finally make our way to Wal-Mart, the blue entrance greeting us. I nod respectfully to the greeter at the front while grabbing a flyer from the wrack to see what's on sale. Reluctantly I release Tate's arm to go and take a shopping cart from the corner. The two of us walk around the grocery section heading in the direction of the snack aisle, standing in front of the products on display.

"What should we get?" He asks with slight confusion, and I laugh, nuzzling his neck gently.

"How about we get some popcorn, chips, chocolate and ice cream?" I list our snack ideas, making it easier to narrow down what we will snack on for the night.

"Okay, baby girl, pick out what you think would be good for tonight then." Tate laughs. I nod and kiss his jaw before turning towards the chips and grabbing two bags of ruffles plain chips and some sour cream and onion dip. I grab three cans of Pringles - two original flavours and one pizza flavour – as an afterthought before we walk further down the aisle to look at chocolate bars.

"What's your favourite chocolate?" I ask, grabbing a bunch of Smarties and Kit Kats.

"I like the dairy milk ones." He answers, his face focusing

on Julia as he takes pictures of her with her stuffed wolf. I nod, grabbing the milk chocolate and cookies and cream before turning to him with a coy smile.

"Maybe we can see what flavours chocolate enhances," I whisper coyly. His eyes slowly darken with my word while his arm snakes around my waist, pulling me closer to his solid body.

"It sounds like we will need more chocolate then." Is his comeback, his voice low and husky when it enters my ear. I giggle and step away from him, grabbing more milk chocolate and cookies and cream bars, my mind racing on what we could do with the sweet substance. With a childish grin on my face, we head over to my favourite aisle, the ice-cream aisle. I select a tub of Chapman's French Vanilla and Mint Chocolate Chip laughing when Tate places a Neapolitan ice cream into the cart, commenting that mixing the three flavours together is 'The bomb dot com babe.'

"Do we have all the snacks we need?" I ask Tate while aimlessly grabbing a bottle of Wal-Mart white wine off the shelf.

"Yes, we do. All we need now are the movies." Tate answers before steering the stroller towards the electronic aisle. We come to a stop in front of the large 'New Release' display. Tate questions which movies I have seen since they came out in theatres, and I answer that I haven't seen any new movies since May. It was hard going to a theatre when running for my and my babies' lives and freedom. This prompted Tate to start picking each and every last movie off the display and putting them into the cart with the snacks, a smile on his face.

"Guess we will be having movie night for a while." He chuckles, coming to kiss me chastely. I couldn't help the bubble of happiness swelling inside me with how pampering Tate is to me. I am happy to be mated to him with how he's protected me and accepted Julia as his. We make our way to the self-checkout, where Tate informs us that he will get the car and bring it to the front entrance of Wal-Mart to make it easier for us, handing me his credit card and telling me the pin before running off in the direction we came from. With a silly grin on my face, I take my time scanning the items, my eyes scanning over two of the movies: *Onwards* and *Maleficent: Mistress of Evil*. These would be the two we watch tonight.

A Wal-Mart employee offers to push the cart outside for me as I finish paying, and I thank her while the two of us exit the automatic doors. Tate comes to a stop just as we reach the edge of the sidewalk and opens the trunk of the jeep, thanking the teen for her help while he puts the bag away. It is mid-afternoon by now, and my stomach started protesting with the need for food, causing my mate to chuckle at me. Deciding to grab lunch, Tate parks the Jeep in the parking lot, and the two of us decide to walk over to the Tim Horton's to grab a quick lunch. There I feed Julia as a couple of elderly ladies comment on how beautiful she is and – adding to Tate's already sky-high ego – saying how she resembles Tate. This must have helped solidify Tate forever being her father, as his eyes beam with pride. Only a few of us would know the truth. Finally finishing our food, we make our way home. Julia snuggled in her car seat with her wolf. We place Julia into her swing the moment we enter our house. I help Tate unload the car and put the ice cream in the freezer right away to freeze once before we consume it.

"So which one do we watch first?" He asks, picking up his coffee as I sip on my white hot chocolate.

"Let's watch *Onwards* first. Since Julia will be with us while we start our movie day, it's only right to do the child-friendly movies first." I say, smiling, walking into the living room where Tate is organizing the movies on the shelf below our T.V.

"Okay, baby, *Onwards* it is." He chuckles out, taking my left hand and kissing it gently.

"We'll watch it on one condition." He smirks, and I tilt my head. He stands slowly, gets down on one knee, and looks up at me with an adoring smile on his face. My heart stops for a moment as he stares into my eyes, with nothing but love displayed directly at me.

"Laina, will you marry me?"

CHAPTER 23

I stand there in our living room, tears forming in my eyes. I know that, to some people, getting engaged within two months of meeting someone would be considered way too fast, but Tate is literally my soulmate, my other half, the person the Moon Goddess paired me with. I felt complete and whole when with him.

"Laina?" Tate's voice wavered slightly, his happy face slowly losing hope, and I realize that I have stood there a few minutes without answering because his proposal left me speechless. Quickly, I nod my head, yes, feeling my tears flow as I jumped into his arms, causing the two of us to tumble to the floor as I kiss all over his face with joy.

"Yes! Always a yes!" I manage to say once my shock was over, and I pull back to kiss him long and passionately. Panting from the kiss, Tate places a beautiful white gold ring with a heart-shaped diamond on my dainty ring finger, with a smile that beams so brightly as if he won the lottery, a gold medal in the Olympics and the Prime Minister Seat of Canada all in one day. Personally, I loved the look of silver, but the metal harms all supernatural, including werewolves, so white gold is a close alternative.

Tate offers to order in some food for dinner while I set about getting the Blu Ray player ready for our movie. My thoughts drifted to the ring as I stare at it, the plans for our wedding already in motion as I smiled happily. I would wait for a bit for our wedding day wanting to settle the matters with Pine Paw first before saying 'I Do' to Tate.

"Penny for your thoughts?" Tate muses, bringing me out of my thoughts as I turned to look at his smiling profile.

"Pennies don't exist in Canada anymore, remember." I laugh, taking the offered wine glass from his hand and sipping on the sweetly-tart goodness.

"Well then, nickel for your thoughts?" He corrects himself, causing me to burst out laughing. I shake my head at my mate's childishness while he joins me to sit on the sofa. If someone told me four months ago that the most-feared wolf next to the Alpha King is a good ball, I would have laughed in their face and walked away.

"So, what were you thinking about?" Tate asks, looking sideways at me. His hand gently pushes Julia's swing now that she has fallen asleep, and a blush creeps along my cheeks.

"Plans for our wedding," I confess, watching his smile grow wide with my words. Every girl had dreams for their wedding day, and I am no exception. I just wanted an amazing day, filled with family and love, something small and intimate and easy to sneak away from once the night ends.

"I know that even in a paper bag, you will be the most beautiful girl that day." He says, taking my hand and kissing the ring. I giggle with his words, taking the time to snuggle into Tate's side with his arms wrapped around me. The fall sunlight filters into the room through the large windows, falling onto Julia, giving our child an ethereal glow. The quiet and cozy atmosphere warming my heart as I watch my little girl sleep soundly.

"I could stay here and watch her forever," I whisper, looking to Tate, who nods and smiles at me before our attention return to our baby girl.

"I could too." He whispers back, kissing the top of my head, making my smile even wider. It felt nice having my small family here with me.

Deciding to wait for Julia to wake up before we watch the first movie, Tate and I turn the T.V. on, surfing the channels until we decided on *Murdoch Mysteries*. Food shortly arrives, and Tate leaves me in the living room while collecting the delivery from the teen. I smell the scent of Indian cuisines as Tate rounds the corner with a large bag setting the contents out on the table as I run into the kitchen to bring out plates and silverware. We continue our show while eating. Something about the Victorian era always bringing out my love for interior design, especially with how *Murdoch Mysteries* is set and designed. Some time into our second episode, with the food eaten and dishes cleared away, Julia decides to voice her complaints.

"I got her," Tate says, getting up and walking to the swing where he lifts our child up, swaying side to side as he soothed her. He takes her upstairs for a diaper change while I make my way to the kitchen to prepare a bottle for our hungry baby. Making sure the bottle is at a perfect temperature, I walk into the living room just as Tate does, handing him the bottle to let my mate feed our daughter.

"Why don't you set up the snacks while I feed our little princess, and we can turn on the movie," Tate suggests. I agree, returning to the kitchen to grab the bag of snacks left on the counter and the Neapolitan and mint chocolate chip ice cream from the freezer. Setting the snacks out on the coffee table, Tate continues to feed Julia as I bustle about choosing the movie Onwards, placing it into the Blu Ray player before settling into the sofa beside Tate, who cradles a wide-awake Julia in his arms.

The movie slowly begins with some laughter coming from me with how the siblings act together, and Tate rolls his eyes.

"This movie is so basic." He grumbles, and I shush him, my eyes taking in everything.

"I like kid's movies; this includes Pixar and Disney films, so shush," I warn, pouting playfully as I snuggle closer. Movies like these always bring out the child inside everyone, leaving a lasting message that shapes children. I much preferred these types of movies to horror or thriller movies.

"Okay, okay." He says in surrender, wrapping his arms around my shoulder pulling me closer to his body. I smile and focus back on the movie, small noises from Julia every now and then coming from Tate's arms, causing us to laugh. As I watch the colourful memories float by, my own heart wrenching when they turn sad as life changed. It reminded me slightly of how mine had changed drastically from losing my parents to becoming an illegal Breeder, gaining a mate worth loving and becoming a mother to my babies, even if all I have is Julia to raise. I stop paying attention to the movie as I fell into my own thoughts, thinking about every last memory I made, all the pain I have been through, and all the happiness that found and lead me to where I am now.

"Baby? Babe? Baby girl?" I blink as I turn to stare at Tate, blushing slightly as I realize that the movie had finished.

"Sorry," I mumble, smiling sheepishly at my mate.

"It's okay. So where did you go?" He says, detangling himself from me to put a sleeping Julia in her swing, setting it on a gentle speed.

"I was thinking about my life. Watching the movie made me realize how much I have been through to get to where I am today." I say quietly, scooting over so that Tate could sit back down, having him pull me close so that our legs were spread out on the couch, his slightly wrapped around mine.

"Want to talk about it?" He asks, one hand playing with my hair, the other rubbing my back.

"I guess." I sigh out, taking a deep breath of his intoxicating scent.

"I never told you much about my parents," I whisper,

clutching his shirt.

"No, but I knew you would in the end." He says, kissing the top of my head.

"I was six when they were murdered. My father was the Beta at the time, and a rogue pack attacked us when we were celebrating his birthday. I was still too young and hadn't shifted yet, so I was rushed into the panic room with the wolves who couldn't fight. When it was over, they were gone." I shuddered as a few tears fell from my eyes, and I bury my face into his chest, taking deep breaths to calm myself.

"I'm sorry, baby." He whispers, kissing my head.

"So am I," I mumbled.

"I never got to say I was sorry to them. That morning I had fought with them about the dress I was wearing, wanting to be in jeans and a tank top so that I could play sports. But my dad argued, saying that the daughter of a Beta should be proper and look like a lady. I ended up saying I hated them, and those were the last words I said to them." By now, I was fully crying as I clutch Tate's shirt. No one knew that the last moments my parents and I had are the ones I regret.

"And you wish you could take it all back." His words were a statement, and I look up to see his face full of understanding.

"Every day of my life." I agree, resting my head in the crook between his shoulder and neck. He nods and hugs me tight as I sniffle, my tears now staining his shirt.

"The last time I saw my parents, I said the same thing, even told them their plane would crash." He admits, and I look up to see him watching me.

"They were on their way to make a treaty with a European pack, and they were missing my first soccer game in high school. They never missed anything when it came to Eeva, but they were busy every time something important to me came up. I felt neglected, and I grew to hate them. Truth is, I still do." I wait silently while Tate clutches me tighter to him, his eyes gaining a faraway look while I wait for him to continue.

"One day, the Beta came to our house, said the plane was shot down by an Asian pack, and there were no survivors. I vowed that day that I would never miss anything my children do. I want to make every day and every memory count." His eyes went cold as he talked about his parents but softened at the end, and I smile, wrapping my arms around his neck and pulling him close for a kiss.

"I love you," I say when we pull away smiling, our foreheads against each other's.

"And I love you too." He says, nuzzling our noses together. Tate later goes to explain that Eeva took over as temporary Alpha until he finished school. At the age of nineteen, he became the youngest Alpha ever. It explains why Tate is so ruthless when he needs to deal with other packs. We decided to continue our movie marathon in bed, Tate bringing the snacks into the room while I settle Julia in bed. I felt our relationship growing closer with our confessions about our parents and sigh. Both of us had the same vow to always be there for our pups and that thought brings a smile to my face.

CHAPTER 24

I shiver slightly as my body slowly comes to consciousness, my eyes scanning the room to see the sunshine falling in through the open window curtains. This morning, the bed felt colder than usual, and my hands search for the warmth Tate always brings. Worried, I turn around to face Tate's side of the bed, only to notice him gone and—judging by how cold his side of the bed is—he's been gone a while.

Frowning, I slowly sit up, my body sore once again from spending the night with my mate. Wrapping the blanket around my naked body, I search for any clue that my mate might have left indicating his whereabouts when I spy the note folded neatly on his pillow.

With a soft smile, I pick up the note and carefully unfold the paper to see Tate's neat handwriting on display. The note tells me that Tate decided to go to the pack house to take care of some business and catch Rex for a check-up. Chris and Jack took Julia for the day, wanting to give me some time to rest and sleep in. Warmth fills my heart with the wonderful family I have. I smile and kiss the note, placing it on the nightstand stationed on my side of the bed before getting up for a quick shower and dressing in a warm baggy knit sweater, fleece-lined leggings and a grey scarf before heading downstairs. Entering the kitchen, I make a quick, light breakfast and take the time to scroll through my phone. I knew I had projects due soon for my courses in college, but those can wait. I wanted to do something fun for myself first.

Taking a look at the calendar, I see that Tate has changed

it from September to October, and an idea came to me. Grinning like a Cheshire cat, I finish my breakfast and make my way to the garage. Texting Tate, I ask where he hides the decorations for Halloween. A quick reply comes, and I giggle first at the picture of him bored out of his mind during a phone call, and then with the information that the decorations are where I am heading. Pressing the button on the side by the garage door, I watch the wind blow leaves across the yard. Deciding on my first chore, I get to work grabbing the rake from the wall and slowly raking the leaves into the middle of the yard on the house's left side. It took a lot longer than I thought it would, but eventually, all the leaves were piled high. Part of me wanted to enclose the area around the pile of leaves, so I lean the rake against the sturdy oak tree and make my way into the large garage. After rummaging around, I find some large fences about a meter tall that can easily be hammered into the ground. I make a couple of trips going back and forth until all the temporary fences are laid out in a large enough area.

Quickly, I fence in the leaves, taking a break once the fencing is done to make a sign with some old wooden boards, paint and nails that read Leaf Jumping Pile that I found in a box by Tate's workbench. I never knew how much of a handyman Tate was until now, and it makes me smile knowing that I had tools readily available for decorating and building. Hammering the sign at the entrance of the fencing, I take a moment to admire my handiwork. I noted that the garden would need some work done. Obviously, the plants have been neglected since first arriving here, so I put myself up to the challenge. Not many people like gardening, but I found the rhythmic action to be soothing and relaxing. I find a yard waste bag and some gloves and set to work in the garden. I trim the bushes and prep the shrubbery for the winter that is fast approaching.

My phone is blaring music from Spotify as I work outside, enjoying the easy exercise gardening brings. It felt nice moving my body again after having a baby and being cooped up, waiting for Tate to wake up from his coma. With a smile, I lean back to rest when my ringtone cuts my music short. Only a few people have my number. Rushing to pick my phone up, I bypass looking at the caller I.D. and just swipe the answer icon.

"Laina here." I greet, heading onto the rocking chair that Tate and I had bought just after being released from my hospital trip.

"Hey, baby, how is your day going?" I smile at Tate's voice, closing my eyes and relaxing as the chair rocks.

"It's going well. I'm decorating the house for Halloween." I answer. My finger slowly moves to play with my engagement ring while Tate chuckles at my enthusiasm.

"There are more decorations in the basement and some in the shed behind the garage once you finish using the ones I keep year-round in the garage. If you need anything else, we can go shopping." I grin at the idea of shopping. I had a feeling that there will be more than enough decorations here at the house, but we could probably have the scariest house on the block if I find things I like.

"That sounds like fun. We can get some costumes too." I agree, giggling. I love Halloween and the idea of dressing up in costume, just being carefree for the day. Part of me preferred going to haunted houses instead of trick or treating like most children would do growing up. It just felt more fun seeing what humans consider scary.

"And what would my baby girl want to be?" I blush at his words and think of Julia, him, and myself, an idea forming.

"Why don't we dress up as a King and Queen and Julia as a princess?" I suggest, hearing another chuckle.

"Okay, but we are not getting cheap Wal-Mart costumes. I have an idea of what we are going to get." He states. We talk for a few more minutes about dinner plans, how the pack business is going. Unfortunately, his break comes to an end too soon, and with a promise to see each other soon, we hang up.

The garden is almost cleaned and ready for winter. I face two large yard waste bags filled to the brim after all that weeding and trimming. If I remembered correctly, tomorrow is garbage day, so doing the gardening today lined up perfectly. Hauling the two bags to the curb, I double-check the front yard before deciding that now will be a good time to start decorating. I start bringing out each and every decoration box, starting from the basement and working towards the ones left in the garage.

It took another hour before I had each box in the garage, a total of ten lined up in a row. Rummaging through each box's contents and organizing the decorations, I find myself with many ideas and categories I can do to make the house the best one on the block. I notice that three boxes contain graveyard materials, and an idea came to mind. A cemetery-themed house would be perfect for children coming to the house for trick or treating.

I soon realize that each headstone is made with Styrofoam covered in concrete as I move them into place, and couldn't help but take the time to read each one when I notice they have a theme. Each headstone contains the name of a book character, some I recognize and others I did not. I found more temporary fences to create a path, zigzagging from the cemetery entrance to the exit that stops just before the front porch. At the end of this path, I set up an automatic coffin that opens with motion sensors to a zombie jumping out. The final touches are solar power lights that light the cemetery path in a red and orange glow. Taking a step back, I take a picture of the house and send it to Tate. I love how it came out and knew that Halloween this year will be the best one yet.

Satisfied with my productive day, I make my way up the driveway, intending to go inside to start dinner. Suddenly the street turns eerily quiet, and unease fills me. Getting ready to run into the house, I feel strong arms wrap around my midsection as another pair presses a cloth with some form of drug to my face, covering my mouth and nose. I try my best to hold my breath in order to not breathe in the drug that threatens to take me into unconsciousness. My hands claw at the ones binding me, trying my best to fight for freedom. I get a few curses of pain in response from the two men holding me captive. I need help and fast.

[Tate help-] I start mind-linking my mate but everything soon turns black as I take a deep breath of air for my burning oxygen-deprived lungs. My body goes slack against the attackers, my arms falling to my side and tears forming in my eyes as I take one last look at the place I call home.

"Good girl." The attacker whispers in a familiar voice, caressing my hair and supporting my limp frame. The last thing I felt is his lips on my temple as my consciousness slips away.

CHAPTER 25

I feel numb as if there were no connection between my mind and body. I feel no emotion, no wave of energy from the pack link, and barely a hum from the mate bond. I am floating in a blissful sleep, or so I think with how the darkness envelops me. My body is numb, yes, but as I open my eyes I soon learn that I am tied down to an all too familiar bed that I thought I left behind months ago, my body naked once again.

"No!" I cry out in a despaired whimper, trying to free my limbs before anyone can walk in. I am back in the cottage I was once sentenced to as a Breeder about five months ago. This is the same cottage where the twins were forcefully conceived, and my life was a nightmare because of Sam for a full week. I was trapped with nowhere to go. The bed is still as comfortable as I remember it, but it holds so many horrible memories that disgust rushes through me in waves.

"Well, look who's up." I bristle as a voice I could never forget floats to my ear, and I growl. I wanted to shift, needed to shift to protect myself and I tried so hard to will my body to cooperate but nothing worked.

[Tate?] I reached out through the bond, trying to reach my mate.

[Please, Tate, answer me.] I beg, looking around to find some way of escape once again.

"It won't work, Laina." Sam's voice cuts through my attempt to link Tate to get help.

"There is currently a low dose of wolfsbane coursing

through your veins." His voice is filled with humour as he steps into my line of sight. I see the triumphant smirk on his lips as his eyes glide over my naked form, lust and greed evident in his brown orbs. I hate this vile man.

"I am a Luna and leader of a pack. You have no right to treat me this way." My voice comes out strong and authoritative as I try to buy time to keep this man away from me. But my outburst only causes a chuckle of amusement from the wolf before me. He steps closer to my body, his hand running from my neck, over the swell of my breast where he plays with my nipple and lowers to trace the entrance of my womanhood. Fear washes over me, but I do my best to hide my emotions. I refuse to give him any satisfaction knowing I am afraid.

"I can do anything I want to you; you're my Breeder, my property." He growls out possessively, his voice low and threatening as his head hovers above mine. He licks his lips as he hooks a finger just inside me, and it takes everything in me not to wince from pain and discomfort.

"I am a free person." I spat out, forcing my head to collide with his as I hear the satisfying crunch of bone. Watching Sam pull back and curse, I catch sight of blood starting to trickle down from his nose. He glares at me, his hand balled into a fist as he raises it into the air and I brace myself for the impact.

"You little-"

"Sam!" He stops as another voice fills the room, turning to snarl at the newest arrival.

"If you want her to produce pups, she needs to be uninjured." I recognize the voice, but I couldn't figure out where it came from. My mind is racing as I try to match this voice to a face.

"Now, go get Doc to look at that nose. We don't want it to heal crooked." The voice continues pacifying the angry Alpha male I have injured.

"Fine, but I get to punish her later, uncle," Sam says, then it hits me. The man is Ross, one of the elders that came to my house weeks ago.

"Fair enough, and when she gives you an heir I call being the next wolf that fucks her. It's been a while since I've been deep inside someone so tender." Ross agrees coming to stand beside Sam and trail his fingers over my breast with lust filling in own eyes. I growl at the two men, trying once again to break free, only to get amused chuckles from these men.

"Don't struggle, Laina. I want this perfect little body under my own, withering at my touch as I fuck you into submission." Sam says, a glint in his eyes as he stares down at me in amusement. Soon, the two leave me alone while Sam tends to his broken nose and Ross goes to Goddess only knows where. I am trapped once again, and I know it, but I need to get out, get to my family, and to safety.

I sigh and close my eyes trying to open the mate bond to reach Tate, but nothing is there. Tears finally formed in my eyes as I think about my mate and our little girl, feeling the ring on my left hand for comfort. At least Sam kept the engagement ring on my hand. My hair flows down my shoulders, covering my mark, and I wonder if this is so that no one sees I am mated. Breeders were supposed to be unmated females in the past. Taking any wolf who bears a mate mark is grounds for execution.

Realizing that I am back in this mess as a hostage now—as nothing more than a vessel to have pups—I let the tears fall. Hope that used to fill me to the brim from the freedom I gained with Tate starts to fade quickly. Unless a miracle happens, I will be trapped here for the rest of my life, never to see Tate, Julia, or anyone else I call family back in Bloodsvain ever again.

I must have dozed off in despair because the sound of the door opening causes me to wake with a start, the binds keeping me in place as I jump in fright.

"Hello, Laina, you look healthy." Doctor Freelan says as he stares at my naked body, his hand resting on my abdomen.

"What do you want?" I growl out, getting a chuckle from him.

"Nothing, just giving you a daily dose of wolfsbane and the special serum you have already been acquainted with before." He replies with a smirk, bringing a needle into view and jabbing it into my arm as he injects the liquid into me. I feel a slight sting from the wolfsbane, causing me to wince. Even in small quantities, this drug can cause harm to a werewolf. I was no exception, as the pain from the injection causes me to whimper.

"Now, relax. You will be feeling good soon. I'll send Sam up in an hour when your body is at its horniest, and you are willing to participate in making our Alpha healthy pups again." With that, he flicks his finger across my breast. I feel nothing but disgust as he chuckles and gets up, walking towards the door and leaving me alone again. I lay here on this bed, feeling the wolfsbane make its way through my body, but nothing else. There is no intense heat like the first time the doctor injected me, no pain because my body craved to be touch, nothing. I smirk.

This could work to my advantage.

Closing my eyes, I decide to rest a little longer, considering the intense heat I expected never came. If there is a way I can uncover my mate mark, maybe I could get free from this predicament quickly. I know Doctor Freelan respected mates and the mate bond, but that's about all that he respects next to the current Alpha.

The door opens again, and I know that an hour has gone by as Sam's musk fills the room. He is undoubtedly horny and ready to take me by force this time.

"How do you feel?" His voice is husky as he tries to seduce me, moving in between my legs, rubbing his tip against my thigh. I don't answer him, my focus moving towards the door as it shuts, the Doctor coming into view.

"Don't worry, Laina, I am here to make sure he doesn't hurt you." Doctor Freelan reassures, taking a seat on the lounge chair beside the door.

"How about you let me go instead!" I say harshly, gasping as I feel Sam push inside me, the pain coursing through my body. It feels like knives are cutting through my insides as I scream, tears streaming from my eyes. "That shouldn't have hurt." Doctor Freelan muses, confusedly, standing to his feet. Sam ignores my pleas for him to stop as blood flows out with each thrust inside me. I wanted this pain to end and prayed for death to take me first. Pushing harder into me, Sam grunts with pleasure as I try my best to thrash around, trying to get him away. I hear Doctor Freelan gasps the moment my hair falls away from my shoulder and onto the bed, revealing Tate's mate mark.

"Samuel, Stop!" Doctor Freelan yells out, rushing towards the end of the bed and dragging Sam away from me. I cry as Sam's length is pulled out of me, feeling the stickiness of blood coating my legs.   "Why did you stop me, Freelan!" Sam growls out, sending a punch across Doctor Freelan's face. I feel the rage simmering off of Sam watching as the doctor tries his best to stand up to Sam.

"Do you know how long I've waited to fuck this bitch? A week! She's been out cold for a week, and no one would let me touch her until she woke up." Sam continues to yell, his eyes turning red from rage. I do my best to make myself appear small, not wanting to catch either man's attention while the ripples of pain slowly die down. I did not want to go through that hell again.

"She is my woman, Freelan. I was there holding onto her body as she cried from her parents' death and knew right then and there I wanted her. On her twelfth birthday, I took her out in a dress that took everything in me not to fuck her in. My father and mother promised me that she would be mine and I would spend every moment with her as she grew up. I took her first kiss. I own her and her little body, and with the blood of Crestfur Alphas running through her, we would have created a stronger pack!" Same rants.

It's true with what he said about taking my first kiss. Chris and Jack had decided that since I was safe with Sam, they took the day to themselves, allowing me to stay at Sam's house that night. I remember being shy since Alpha Blake and Luna Rose were out on pack business. Sam and I spent the night after returning to the pack in his room, with me wearing one of his large T-shirts as a nightshirt. We were watching the Titanic when I felt his eyes on me, and as I turn to face him, his lips found mine. He went slowly at first, his hands wrapped around my waist until I found myself underneath him with his tongue swirling around my mouth and his hand groping my blooming chest. He promised not to go far as I was too young to be mated, but at the time, I remember him sticking my hand deep into his pants, showing me how to move as he continued to make out with me. Every now and then since that night, Sam would send me an outfit to wear—outfits that I now realize revealed too much skin for a young pup—and would take me out only for the night to end with us making out. It's why I always believed we were mates, that he knew from the beginning that I was his soulmate. Now I know that he was just grooming me to be his Breeder and sex toy to play with. This man is sick and used me as his own play toy, and I played right into his hands the day he made me a Breeder.

"I stopped you because she is mated. There is a reason why Breeders are un-mated females. If a mated female is touched in any sexual way, the action will kill her. That is why she is bleeding!" Doctor Freelan states, doing his best to hold Sam back from my body. Sam just scoffs at his words as his eyes rake over me once again, his reaction causing Doctor Freelan to gasp in a mix of horror and shock.

"But you knew that already." He gasps out, walking backwards to stand between Sam and me, shielding my body from the angry Alpha wolf before us.

"Who is her mate Samuel Lightran?" The Doctor demands just as the door shatters open.

"I am."

CHAPTER 26

"I am." I smile despite the pain as Tate's voice reaches my ear, my heart soaring at the fact that my mate is here to save me. I turn my head to look at Sam, his face a ghostly white, and I smile smugly. He is in a world of pain for pissing off my mate and kidnapping me.

"Sam! Bloodsvain, they're here." I hear Ross's words of warning as he yells out to his nephew. I hear the Elder's heavy steps from the hallway carrying him into the room, where he abruptly comes to a stop.

"Oh, Alpha Tate, how-" I hear a growl cutting off Ross' sweet, fake greeting before the sound of flesh tearing apart and the smell of blood other than my own fills the air. *Guess there will be an Elders position to fill soon.*

"Look, Tate, I was just taking back what is mine," Sam says with fear lacing his voice. Holding his hands in surrender, Sam slowly backs away from the bed and away from me, with Doctor Freelan continuing his protective stance, just in case Sam tries anything stupid. Tate slowly comes into view, his body splattered with blood but still so sexy. I've missed my mate so much.

"You okay, baby girl?" Tate asks, his eyes never leaving Sam's face. I feel the rage simmering around Tate's body, and I knew that by the time we leave this territory, there will be no more Pine Paw in the werewolf world.

"No, I'm not. I just want to be untied and go home." I answer. Tate gives Doctor Freelan a look, and the wolf soon busies himself by untying the knots that hold me tight. Even though I hate this wolf before me for drugging me for once, I allow his touch as it brings me closer to freedom. Once all the ropes are untied, I slowly sit up with the help of Doctor Freelan, who backs away from me respectfully, his head bowed.

"I didn't know you were mated. If I knew, I would have stepped in." Doctor Freelan says remorsefully. But his remorse would not save him as Tate reaches out and clutches his throat. I focus on massaging my sore wrists and ankles, now robbed raw from the ropes that were discarded in a heap. No sounds come from Doctor Freelan, but I knew better than to look as the sounds of flesh once again tearing from another body resounds in the room. The loud sound of Freelan's dead body hitting the ground echoes, causing a panic-stricken look on Sam's face. His body is next, and I anticipate the moment when he takes his last breath.

Tate moves quickly like a fluid dancer. The sound of bones crunching brings to my attention that he has broken Sam's nose in the span of a second. My eyes watch each movement my mate makes as he lands punch after punch to Sam's face, seeing for once the blood-thirsty Alpha mothers use to scare their pups into behaving. Sam cries out in pain, falling to his knees and causing the swell of happiness inside me to see him suffer. He deserves it.

Attempting to stand, Sam lets out a fierce growl through his rearranged face. It is evident that his nose and jaw are broken allowing his blood to drip down his chin and onto the hardwood floor. I watch Sam rushing towards Tate like a wounded, rabid animal taking a final stand against an apex predator. But Tate just scoffs at Sam's measly attempt as he dodges the weaker wolf. Sam's movements become frantic while trying to claw at my mate, but his movements are slow, as if he is put into slow motion when faced against Tate. I could tell that Tate's focus is to draw Sam away from me as they near the window on the opposite side of the room.

With one last attempt at a successful attack, Sam lunges into the air only for Tate to use his own momentum and sending Sam crashing into the window as his body pauses in midair before falling two stories onto the waiting concrete below.

I blink, stunned at how Sam's fate has turned out.When I open my eyes, Tate is beside me, pulling me into his strong arms and kissing me passionately. Gone is the cold, distant man from before, reverting back into the loving mate I have gotten to know. His blood-covered body coats the sticky red substance onto my naked one while our lips smash together for a few more seconds before we pull away, panting.

"Baby, I've missed you." He whimpers, tears now flowing from his eyes, once cold-hearted, murdering Alpha eyes now softening in a way only the pack and I would know. His forehead is pressed against my own while his body shakes with quiet sobs. He felt so fragile in my arms.

"I've missed you too," I whisper, my own tears falling from my face.

"It's been a long week looking for you and getting the attack ready." Tate whisper, and I stiffen.

"It's been a week?" I ask shakily with the realization. I knew Sam was rambling on about me being asleep, but I was too focused on the crippling pain to notice what he was saying.

"Yes, baby, that's how long you were gone. He had you for a week, and I spent every day trying to follow protocol before I was finally able to be let loose. How long did you think it was?" His face is filled with confusion while I clutch his shirt, my own tears flowing faster as sobs wrack my body.

"I thought it has only been a day!" I exclaim, my heart wrenching at the fact that I was here for a week and I didn't know it.

"Why would you-" He stops and sniffs my body and

frowns as he wraps the blanket around me gently. I still felt weak and groggy from the drugs that have been used to incapacitate me.

"They used wolfbane on you." He growls out. I can only answer with a nod, seeking comfort in his arms as I continue to sob. I want to go home now.

"It explains why I couldn't reach you and why you wouldn't know it's been a week." He adds as he lifts me up gently. His arms cradle me close to his chest while he stands, turning towards the empty door frame.

"Alpha Tate, we have Samuel in custody." As Mike comes into view, I look despite the blurry vision, catching him take in the blood-soaked floors and broken window. He doesn't seem fazed by the blood covering Tate while he sends a reassuring smile my way.

"Glad to see you're safe, Luna Laina." He adds, bowing his head and moving out of the way to let Tate pass by with me in his arms.

"I would say have a clean-up crew in here, but instead, I want you to burn this place down. I need to get Laina to Rex." Tate orders, his hold on me tightening. I can feel his swirling emotions radiating off of him, and I kiss his mark, trying to calm my mate down. Mike nods in acknowledgement while Tate carries me down the stairs, where more bodies litter the floor with puddles of blood pooling below them. As we near the front door, the body count increases, with many of them in wolf form.

"They tried to stop me from rescuing you," Tate informs me, and I smile, his eyes catching my curious gaze. I felt no fear knowing the damage my mate has caused instead, I kiss his blood-stained cheek and smile lovingly at him.

"You came for me. That is all that matters to me." I reassure Tate and snuggle into his embrace. Walking past the house, he carries me down the street where our pack guards line the pavement until I find ourselves entering a field of wild-flowers. Tents and vans scatter the field as make-shift medical tents with a few wolves seeking treatment. It seems like there were no casualties from Bloodsvain, and I smile in relief. I hated the thought of pack members dying for my sake. Rex spots us from his van as he sets up materials for the next patient, his eyes lighting up in happiness and relief before he rushes to our side and giving me a quick once-over before we make our way towards his van. Tate sets me down gently on a metal table, making sure the blanket is wrapped around my body, keeping me warm from the cold fall wind.

"We have all the wolves from Pine Paw, pups included, in their pack house. Loren is watching over them with a few of our Warriors." Rex informs the both of us, putting on a pair of rubber gloves and readying his medicine.

"Good, we can take care of them soon. Laina has wolfsbane in her system. Do you think you can treat her?" I allow Tate to speak for me, my body becoming heavy with exhaustion as I fight to stay awake. It's been a long day, and the idea of sleeping tucked safely beside Tate tempted me. Rex does a quick exam, giving me some medication for the pain and informing Tate that he was lucky he came when he did. I had to whisper out that Sam raped me and that Freelan had stepped in just in time, causing a loud, blood-curdling growl to settle over the field from Tate, his eyes fighting to not turn red.

"Laina will be fine, Tate. The wolfsbane will need a few days to exit her system, but it's nothing that will cause lasting damage." Rex states with an exasperated sigh, sending a small smile my way. I nod in acknowledgement at his words as I reach my hand out from under the blanket to clutch Tate's feeling my mate visibly relax. I see relief in Rex's eyes, probably because I stopped him from going rampant, before nodding for Rex to continue speaking.

"You can take her home after we deal with Pine Paw and

Samuel. You have the go-ahead from the Elders to do as you please with him." Rex continues with a smirk, a tinge of blood-thirstiness coming from the Doctor.

"My thoughts exactly! Sam will pay for what he's done." Tate agrees, kissing my forehead. Rex begins packing away his medical materials into the trunk whole my mate scoops me up into his arms, once again, climbing into the back of the vehicle and clutching me to him. I couldn't help but sigh as familiar tingles spread from where his skin touches mine and close my eyes for a moment. The sound of the driver door chimes with the door opening. Rex climbs in and turns the ignition, and in moments, the car moves. Leaving behind the Breeder Lane, the car turns onto a familiar road that will take us to the pack house.

I watch as houses pass by, and the territory I used to run in brings back old memories. But Pine Paw is no longer my home, and the feeling of being here makes my skin crawl with unease. I doze off on the drive to the pack house, only to be gently awoken with a kiss from Tate, a soft smile on his face.

"It's cold out, baby, so put this on. It's one of the shirts you like to steal from me." My heart flutters with the care from my mate as I let the blanket slide off my shoulder, and Tate helps me dress. The long sleeve shirt is comfortable baggy, and as I am helped by Rex to exit the van, the shirt falls almost to my knees. The warmth of the blanket is wrapped around me again by Tate blocking out the cold October wind. Members of our pack line the entrance and perimeter of Pine Paw's pack house, giving off an intimidating aura, but I catch the look of relief in their eyes. Nodding to the wolves we pass, our trio make its way into the pack house, walking side-by-side to the grand ballroom.

The first thing my eyes zero in on is the beaten and battered body of Sam on the center of the stage. He is tied to a sturdy metal chair, slumped over in defeat while blood drips from his wounds and two guards on either side of him—one I recognize as Alex. It is evident that bones are broken as one of Sam's legs is at an odd angle, but I feel nothing for this wolf other than hate and disgust. Part of me had hoped he had died from his fall out of the window. But he will be dead before we leave; I just had a feeling of it.

"You monster..."

"He is our Alpha..."

"Why do you always kill packs..."

The crowd of Pine Paw wolves yell in anger and frustration with the heavy scent of fear emanating in the air. I could see mothers holding their pups close to their bodies while guards create a path for us to walk through, Rex falling back to walk behind us. Abby's face catches my attention as she stares wide-eyed at me, her mate being detained on stage behind his Alpha, but I ignore the two-faced bitch. As far as I am concerned, she lost the right to be my friend months ago, and her tear-stained face brings no sympathy for her from me. Taking a spot slightly to the left of Sam, I stand as straight as I can, putting on a brave front and waiting for the crowd to settle down. The four remaining Council of Elders members join us, standing to Sam's right, a look of disgust on their faces as Dian sends me a relieved smile. She is definitely my favourite Elder.

"Let me explain what is going on here." Tate starts off with once there is silence in the room.

"Your Alpha here has been creating illegal Breeders for his own gain, and Laina, my mate, was forced to be one about seven months ago." Confused murmurs follow Tate's words with this new revelation. It seems like no one knew the truth about Breeders being illegal. Well, not no one, as Abby's face holds a guilt-stricken look. I know instantly that she knew about this and still allowed me to be one.

"Laina ran away a week after Sam forced himself on her in hopes of creating heirs since he had no mate. About seven weeks ago, she ran into my territory where we learned we are mates, and a week ago, Sam kidnapped her, knowing full well she was mated to me. He forced himself on her, nearly killing my mate." Tate continues as gasps of horror fill the air. I see wolves pulling their mate to their sides protectively as their eyes turn to me. I make sure my mate mark is displayed fully for all to see and nod to reaffirm Tate's words. I could see the crowd warming up to my mate and gently reach out to squeeze Tate's hand.

"We also know that Mr. Samuel knew that Breeders were illegal but continued the practice anyways for two years after the law was passed, breaking the laws that we, the Elders, created to protect our kind." Dian states and the crowd breaks out into outraged cries.

"Wait, you're saying that Breeders are illegal now?" A she-wolf asks, pushing to the front of the crowd to search for answers from the Elders.

"They were made illegal over two years ago due to the fact of the trauma the girls went through. Samuel attended the meeting that day with his Beta and Beta Female when we talked to all the North American Alphas and Betas, yet he chose to ignore our laws and continue without informing all of you." Another Elder says, and the crowd grows angry once again, this time at the man they thought was a trustworthy Alpha. I feel a rise in bloodlust emanating from some of the crowd members, catching Alex stiffening. As a child of a Breeder himself, I have a feeling Alex is ready to rip Sam apart.

"It is why we give Tate Randall-Silvermoon permission to kill him in front of you, the pack members of Pine Paw, since Samuel and Samuel's close guards attacked his pack, and since his mate, Laina, the Luna of Bloodsvain, was kidnapped and violated by Samuel." Dian continues, giving Tate a nod of approval to go ahead with this execution. The crowd roars for the kill, and Tate grins as he kisses my forehead before walking to Sam. Fear radiates once again from the wolf tied down to the chair, with Sam giving pleading looks for his freedom. No amount of pleading will save Sam from his fate.

Tate begins by giving a light kick to Sam's broken leg, causing Sam to groan in pain. The sound of skin ripping away as my mate tears off the broken leg silences the crowd. Blood gushes from the wound where the limb once connected as the dull thud echoes on stage, with Tate discarding the useless limb. Next came an arm that is torn away quickly, causing the crowd to cheer at the strong scent of blood filling the air. Fingers turn to claws, and Tate reaches out, shredding the now limp penis that Sam used to violate me. The blood-curdling scream from the broken wolf sends waves of satisfaction through me. He deserves this, and I am proud my mate got to be the one to make Sam impotent.

Finally with Sam getting close to death from blood loss, Tate comes to stand behind Sam, his hands reaching around to slowly tear the head from Sam's shoulder. The screams stop, and silence resumes with the death of Sam. He would no longer be able to hurt another she-wolf again.

The crowd cheers the death of Sam, as his Beta is brought in front of the crowd, and Abby is dragged to kneel beside her mate. They were accomplices in creating new Breeders, knowing that they were illegal. Their death will be handled by Pine Paw.

"Laina, please help me!" Abby cries out, pleading towards me. I turn a deaf ear to her pleas while the she-wolf struggles to break free from her captors. Instead, I focus on my mate, who wraps me in a hug. I find myself being lifted into his strong arms once again being carried out of the pack house I plan to never set foot in again. Pine Paw can burn for all I care after today. Entering the van with Rex the driver once again, I settle into Tate's lap, my head resting against his shoulder with a yawn.

"Laina Randall-Silvermoon." I say, testing my soon-to-be last name on my lips and smile a drowsy smile.

"Wolf shield of the silver moon." I translate the last name

with a grin, sending a kiss to Tate's mark before yawning once again. Tate chuckles at my sleepy words, kissing my temple and playing with my hair, lulling me to a comfortable sleep now that I am once again safe beside him.

CHAPTER 27

It took us forty-eight hours to return to our pack, despite Rex driving faster than the speed limit permitted to distance ourselves from Pine Paw. Tate wanted to keep driving all through the night, but Rex suggested we stay at a motel the first night because of the condition my body is in due to the wolfsbane. And so, with reluctance, Tate agreed to Rex's suggestion. Settling into a comfortable room, I spent the night dozing in and out of sleep, not able to fully find the release of a deep slumber even with my battered and exhausted body. Every time I would fall asleep, I would find myself back in the cottage with Sam above my body that is chained to the familiar wooden bed. Each time that scene repeated itself, I would scream awake from the nightmare, waking Tate, who slept beside me and sending him into a panic state as he holds me close until my sobbing ends.

After going through ten nightmares, Tate decided that it would be best to leave the motel and continue to drive home. He refused to let me be alone for a second as I spent the majority of the drive in his lap with his fingers running through my hair. His touch made me feel safe and secure, long enough to get some sleep and keep the nightmares at bay for a few brief moments. The only time away from him during our mad drive home would be when we stopped to grab gas and snacks, and I would excuse myself to use the lady's room. Tate's main priority was caring for me, his mate. With the security of being by his side and the closer we were to home, I fell into a deep, dreamless sleep without nightmares interrupting me.

The vehicle coming to a stop, and the tingles of a gentle kiss on my lips wake me from my slumber. Groggily, I look around, noticing the familiar street and our home still decorated for Halloween. Tears of joy fill my eyes and slowly trickle down my face while strong arms pull me in for a long hug.

"Good morning, baby girl, welcome home," Tate whispers, kissing the top of my head and giving me a reassuring smile. The door opens, with Rex greeting us as Tate climbs out of the van, still carrying me. The autumn wind breezes by, causing me to shiver from the cold even with the blanket wrapped around me. Taking in the familiar scents and the decoration that I spent a whole day setting out, I try my best to stifle my relieved sobs.

I am home.

Tate rushes us inside, the warm air embracing me as I take in the scent of our home, closing my eyes and opening again to make sure this wasn't a dream. The scent of Tate and I are stale, but Julia's is still fresh in the air as well as Chris and Jack. Right now, the house held no sounds except the two of us breathing. I was happy with having just Tate and I home, not wanting to deal with a crowd of people.

"Can we go for a shower together? I just need to wash the memories away, and it just to be us for the moment. Please, Tate, help me forget, baby." I ask quietly, my voice pleading for my mate to take away the horrible experience and love me. I rest my head on Tate's shoulder and kiss his mark. I need his touch and love right now. I need my mate.

"Sure, sounds like a good idea." He answers, carrying me up the stairs and into our bedroom past our comfy bed and to the bathroom, where he sets me down on the marble counter with a chaste kiss. Turning away from me to start the shower, I watch Tate's body move to complete the task. I drop the blanket from around me and carefully remove the long sleeve shirt from my body, watching as Tate also removes his blood-soaked clothing. I will ask him to have everything covered in blood taken away later and burned, not wanting any memories of Pine Paw left in our home. Tate turns to face me, a smile on his face after checking the temperature of the water.

"Come here, baby." He whispers, opening his arms, and I hop down from my perch, taking those few steps into those safe, familiar arms and burying my face into his chest—the only part that didn't have blood on him.

"Anything you want to do today, we'll do. Don't worry about our pup. Eeva has Julia for the day to give you some time to relax." He whispers, his face buried in my hair, taking in my scent. I feel each of his muscles relax a little more with each deep breath he takes, his arms pulling me even closer to him. This past week without me must have been hard on Tate, and I could only imagine the worry and anxiety he's gone through with me kidnapped and taken away.

"Okay," I mumble into his warm skin, kissing it gently before I pull away.

"Now, let's get cleaned up," I add with a giggle as I step into the warm spray, Tate following me in soon after. The water started to turn red from all the blood. I grabbed a bar of soap, lathering Tate with it, and massaged the soap into his body until all the blood was gone, and, finally, he stood clean before me. Even his soft hair is free of blood after a long shampoo. I could see the exhaustion and dark circle under his eyes, my heart throbbing with a slight pain, knowing he did not get much sleep. We both needed some pampering with each other later.

"My turn to clean you, sweetheart." He announces playfully, taking the soap and putting it on the built-in shower shelf beside him before spinning me around and washing my hair. I smiled as his fingers massage my scalp, leaning my head back and closing my eyes as he rinsed the chestnut locks clean. He repeats his movements with conditioner, and when I thought he was going to rinse it out, he pulls my hair to the side, letting the strands soak up the condition and massages soap into my back, getting stiff, tensed muscles I didn't know I had until his expert hands found them.

Finally he rinses my hair when he removes the soap suds from my back. I try to turn and face him, but he stops me, pulling my clean back flush against him as his soapy hands massage the top of my chest and shoulders. He trails his fingers along my sides over to my stomach before returning to cup my breast, where he massages the skin clean, gently tugging and pinching my nipples, causing a flushed heat of pleasure to shoot through my body as I let out a slow sensual moan. His lips press against my neck where my mate mark is situated, his teeth gently nipping at the sensitive skin, causing my knees to weaken.

"What do you say we go and have some adult fun after our shower, and I show you how much I worship not only you but your body, mind, and soul as well?" He whispers seductively into my ear, nipping my ear lobe gently.

"I say hurry up and get me clean then," I reply back, my voice laced with lust as my arm snakes up and around his neck. The rest of the shower is a soapy blur as he moved as fast as he could to get me clean, wrapped a towel around our bodies and grabbed a few more that he splayed across the bed before depositing me in the middle. He finds his place between my legs and massages the tip of his hard cock against me, making me moan again as need built.

He takes his time, though, kissing every inch of my body, suckling my breasts as his fingers found a steady rhythm inside me. He kisses his way down my body and swaps his fingers for his tongue, licking and tasting me until I came, screaming his name as I grip the wet towels. When I came back down from the euphoric high, I find him between my legs, smirking as he spreads them wider with his tip against my wet entrance.

"Ready?" He asks playfully, and I smile.

"For you, always." He chuckles at my sweet reply and

slowly pushes inside me, my moan of pleasure mixed with his as he fits perfectly inside. The base of his cock is pressed to my wet lips as he grinds against me for a few minutes, my body tensing from the pleasure he was building. Finally, he starts moving. My legs wrap around his waist as he starts a slow thrust, building up the speed until he was bent over, nipping my neck and amplifying the pleasure as he bites down on my mark, thrusting hard and fast into me. More orgasms rip through my body as I clutch and claw at his back and shoulders, finding my release screaming his name, and hearing him moan mine.

Finally, I feel him tense above me, and the spot he has been favouring on my neck heats up where he bites down once again. The sensation makes me tumble over the edge of ecstasy with him. His seed spills into me as I bite down on the base of his neck, where his mate mark already resides, the mate bond strengthening further. We lay there panting, myself curled into his side, the towels now on the ground as the blanket covers us, and I smile. *This is where I belong.*

"I love you, Tate," I whisper, drawing small circles on his chest.

And I love you, Laina." He whispers back, pulling me closer to him. Soon his breathing evens out, and I look up to see him fast asleep. I giggle, snuggling into him and joining him for much-needed rest.

CHAPTER 28

I groan as harsh light reaches my eyes. My reaction to bury my face in the warm, solid body next to me is met by chuckling. Sometimes I feel more like a vampire with how much I hate the bright star when sleeping.

"Hey, beautiful, are you hungry?" Tate asks, one hand rubbing my back, the other in my hair.

"Yes," I mumble, snuggling closer to him and sighing happily, getting another chuckle.

"Well, we should get up to get food." He says, smoothing my hair away from my face and kissing the top of my head.

"Do we have to?" I ask quietly, blinking my blurry, sleep-filled eyes at him with a yawn.

"You're adorable when you're tired, you know that?" He muses, sending another kiss to my forehead and pulling me closer into his arms.

"So I've been told," I mumble and smile at another deep chuckle rumbling from my mate. It felt good seeing Tate relaxed and a little rested, with the dark circles under his eyes less noticeable.

"C'mon, baby girl. Let's get dressed and make something to eat." He says encouragingly, moving out from under me and causing my body to lie in an uncomfortable position.

"Fine." I groan, stretching out my sore body as I stand and head to the closet, grabbing a simple cotton bra and panties set, a pair of hip-hugging jeans, and a tank top, throwing a soft, long beige cardigan on top. I brush my long hair and tie it in a simple braid, turning around and coming face-first into Tate's chest as he pulls me in for a hug.

"I forgot to give you this." He says, steadying me with one arm around my waist while holding out my phone.

"Thank you, I must have dropped it at some point," I reply, happily taking the device and tucking it into my pocket.

"It was on the ground by the edge of the road." He whispers, his grip tightening on me, and I knew what he was talking about. My heart aches to look into his pain-filled eyes, and I press closer into his body.

"Baby, I'm home safe and sound and in your arms. Everything is fine now, and we have nothing to worry about. I'm here, and I am not leaving." I say soothingly, pressing my hand against his cheek and kissing him lovingly.

"Besides, we have a wedding to plan," I add when we pull away, getting his breath-taking smile and a deep chuckle as his free hand lands on mine cupping his face.

"I know, baby. Now, let's get you some food." He whispers as my stomach growling to punctuate his words, making me giggle. We make our way down to the kitchen, and I flip the T.V. on, going through the guide to see what we can watch until I find *Burlesque* about to play and put it on. Tate has ingredients for a late brunch: bacon, eggs, hash browns, and a fruit salad needing to be prepped. The two of us head to the kitchen counter and start cooking. I promptly begin singing along to all the songs at the start of the film and dancing around happily.

"You seem to know the movie pretty well." Tate comments after the third song, *Diamonds are a Girl's Best Friend*.

"I know the dances as well." I retort with a wink, flipping a few pieces of bacon.

"This I have to see." He chuckles, leaning against the counter with his arms crossed over his chest.

"Depends on how sore my muscles are," I say coyly, smiling when he moves to wrap his arms around me from behind.

"Well, then they are going to be sore for a while." He whispers, nipping my mark and causing me to moan as his lips leave soft kisses trailing along my neck and shoulder.

"Food first, then we figure out what to do afterwards," I say, my breath coming out in pants.

"Okay, baby." He laughs and starts dishing everything out as I plop the last piece of bacon on a paper towel-lined plate. We sit and relax, munching on our brunch-side by-side in the breakfast nook, snuggling and taking our time to enjoy the movie as it gets to the best parts.

"So, what's the story behind this movie?" Tate finally asks, and I giggle.

"It's a musical, basically. Small town girl trying to make it in L.A. in a classy strip club called a Burlesque club. I grew up watching it with Chris because it's a really good movie. I got into dancing because of this, and Chris was more than happy at the time to see me go to the local dance hall in town by the pack." I state, and he whistles, impressed by my confession.

"So you are an interior designer, an artist, a dancer, and have a killer voice! What can't you do, beautiful? " I blush with Tate's impression of me, taking a sip of the orange juice, thinking of the embarrassing things I cannot do. Deciding on the one thing I know I am horrible at, I look to Tate with a dead-serious look.

"Write. My stories are so horrible, and I give up." I deadpan, blushing slightly from my confession.

"That's okay. You're perfect the way you are." He assures me, kissing my forehead.

"And so are you," I say quietly, kissing his chin. The stubble tickles my face, making me giggle. He smirks, and I feel his hands on my sides before I start wiggling around, laughing out loud from the tickle attack as I try to squirm out of his grasp.

"B-baby s-stop." I yelp, panting as I manage to slip away from him, rushing to the other side of the table.

"Oh no you don't, missy!" Tate exclaims, getting up and making me squeal in surprise as I jump out of his reach, bolting for the door. I slip on some black flats and race outside while laughing. I could hear my mate laughing behind me as he chases after my fleeing frame, causing me to laugh even louder. I run through the makeshift cemetery and out towards the leaf pile, squeaking when I feel his strong arms wrap around me and lift me over his shoulder, spinning me around.

"I caught you." He chuckles, spanking my ass, which makes me jump in surprise while laughing.

"No fair, I haven't been able to train." I fake whine and pout as I turn to look at his bemused face.

"I know, but don't worry, baby; I don't mind being the protector." He retorts with confidence before biting my ass playfully, making me giggle. Slowly I feel myself being lowered to the ground, my arms wrapping around Tate's neck and his around my waist as we stand there, our foreheads pressed together.

"I love you." He says tenderly, and my heart melts.

"I love you too," I whisper, giggling when he bites my nose playfully. We play in the leaves for a while, acting like children and letting the tension that has built up over the last few days fully melt away. It felt good being carefree with my mate, not having to worry about our pup or the dangers of Pine Paw lurking in the back of our minds. After a well-needed leaf fight, Tate and I lay snuggled together on the leaf-covered ground watching the clouds float by.

"So for the wedding, when do you want to have it?" He asks, playing with my hair.

"Some time in the spring under all the cherry blossom trees we have in the backyard," I answer quietly, loving the feel of his hands in my hair as usual.

"Sounds good. Do you want to wait a few years before we tie the knot?" He asks, smiling down at me, and we lay there quietly. I nod in response, resting my head on his shoulder and closing my eyes to take in the fall scent mixed with my mate's. We were already mated, so we had no need to rush for the wedding—the engagement ring reminding me that Tate and I were already together and meant to be for eternity.

We head back inside a few minutes later, making a quick dinner and snuggling up on the couch to watch another movie on Netflix, barely paying attention to the T.V. as the two of us talk and relax. Eeva arrives at around eight at night with Julia in her pink stroller, a relieved look on my sister-in-law's face as she hands a box filled with cheesecake to Tate and wraps me in a hug. I smile with the love she radiates for me while she holds me at arms-length.

"Glad to see you home safe and sound, Laina." She whispers with tears of joy in her eyes.

"So am I." The three of us head into the kitchen as I hold Julia in my arms, taking in my pup's sweet scent and closely holding her. I've missed my daughter so much. With a grin on my face, I take a seat, relishing in as much mommy-daughter time as I can while Eeva cuts the cheesecake and Tate pours us all a cup of hot chocolate.

I get caught up on the things Julia has done in my absence, smiling with the news that she is starting to sleep through the night, as well as how Eeva's boys have treated their little cousin. The night ends with Eeva telling us she is pregnant, hoping for a baby girl, before leaving Tate, Julia, and me alone. With my little girl already fast asleep, Tate moves a bassinet to my side of the bed where I lay my baby down and tuck her in before climbing into bed and cuddling with Tate, his warm body and secure embrace helping me fall into another deep sleep.

CHAPTER 29

I smile as I stare at myself in the mirror, my chestnut hair in loose curls, half of it shaped into a bow at the back, upper-half of my head. It's been just over two—almost three—years since I returned home, and news about the fight at Pine Paw has spread all over the world. The Elders visited every single pack for three months, making sure everyone knew the new laws of Breeders being illegal. Many packs were abolished for breaking the laws. The last I heard about Pine Paw is that Sam's younger brother Eric and his mate took over, freeing all the Breeders and reuniting them with their pups. All in all, my story is widely known now. I have a strong reputation of being a kind Luna but a brutal fighter when it comes to protecting my pack and family.

"Are you almost ready?" Eeva's voice fills my ears, and I turn to stare at my maid of honour, smiling at the look of awe on her face as Julia toddles around us in her lavender flower girl dress.

"Yes, is everyone here?" I ask, smoothing the front of my dress gently. Today is my wedding day, and I'm wearing a Pnina Tornai strapless ball gown with a bejewelled, sweetheart neckline. Once my mother's, my veil hangs down just inches above the floor attached to a tiara situated on the top of my head. For the time being, the veil is flipped back, away from my face. I really can't wait to see my mate. The night alone in my cousin's house with Julia was excruciating, and even though I knew it would only be a few hours, I still miss Tate and yearn to be curled beside him on our bed.

"They are all seated and waiting for the three of us. You

look beautiful, by the way, sis." She gushes, and my already pink cheeks turn a deeper shade while Eeva picks up my daughter. Eeva had started calling me sis or little sis just a few months after my return home. It made me happy but irritated Tate to no end. About a year ago, she had given birth to my niece Lora and worked hard to fit into her lavender bridesmaid gown. I couldn't help but chuckle as she twirls around the room with a giggling Julia, who squeals out a "Mommy, help me," then rushes to hide behind my leg the moment Eeva sets Julia on her feet again.

"Thank you," I whisper, watching as another figure walks through my door, Chris stopping dead in his tracks as he takes me in.

"Wow, Lainy, your parents would be so proud." He whispers, using his usual nickname for me as tears threatening to spill from both our eyes. I sniffle a bit, holding back the tears that threaten to spoil my makeup. I walk towards Chris and give him a tight hug. I take in his lavender suit, as he will be walking on my side of the ceremony as my bride's man. I smile at the man who raised me most of my life.

"I know they would, but having you here is just as important," I say, sniffling as I try to keep the tears at bay. I see tears slip from Chris's eyes as he dabs a handkerchief at the drops, causing me to laugh at his emotional state.

"Look, both of you need to hurry up before we're late for a very important date." Eeva huffs with a glare, pushing us towards the door with Julia situated on her right hip.

"Really, *Alice in Wonderland* quotes?" I laugh out, my mood lightening.

"Yes, now move, or else my brother will storm up here and grab you himself if you don't get out there." She adds, and I knew she was right. As quickly as I could in three-inch heels, I make my way down the stairs and out the house with my bouquet of fall flowers in hand. Chris sets my veil over my face before I step outside.

Tate and I had decided to marry each other on the day we met instead of the spring wedding I always dreamed of, but I wouldn't change this date for anything else. It was the day my life changed for the better. Since my cousin's house is close to mine and Tate's, we decided on a backyard wedding, so all I had to do was walk through the forest. The steady march of *"Here Comes the Bride"* plays as I near the edge of the trees, and the guests stand from their chairs while Julia makes her way towards her father in her flower girl outfit. I knew that I was the blushing bride, but as soon as my eyes met Tate's stare full of love, everything stopped, and it was just him and I. No one else mattered as I stood in front of him. My bouquet passed to Eeva as we stood on the gazebo, the water lapping slightly in the surprisingly warm early fall weather.

The preacher started the traditional way to any wedding, no one got up to object, and we continued marching forward.

"A wedding is a joyous event in any love, but a wedding between mates is momentous, and I ask that the Goddess bless them and their family and friends." I smile as my eyes focus on Tate, his own orbs never leaving mine as the preacher continued. Soon the rings were passed to us, and we started our vows, with Tate going first.

"Laina, I knew since the moment I saw you that you were my everything. You make me a better man and gave me a chance to be an amazing father. Even though it's been three years since we met, I know that I never want to lose you, and I will cherish you and our children for the rest of my life. I love you, baby girl."

Tears of happiness start flowing, and I giggle when he wipes them away while ignoring his own tears to tend to mine. He pulls me close, burying his face into the crook of my neck as he cries. Everyone in the room looks shocked, but I smile warmly. I wrap my arms around my mate, smiling at knowing that he is only this emotional around me. The two of us silently cry in each other's embrace. Minutes pass until we calm down, with me wiping away his tears and him wiping away mine. We laugh at each other when the minister motions for us to continue the ceremony.

"Tate, you are my everything, my best friend, my knight in fluffy fur-" That last part has everyone laughing, including Tate, and my smile widens as I take his hands into mine and continue.

"- You're the father of our daughter and my other half. I won't lie and say that I wasn't terrified when I met you because I was. But as I got to know you, I learned you have a softer side, a side only those who are close to you know. I am happy to know I am the one who gets to wake up to you each morning, to smile and laugh and cry with you. I love you, baby, and nothing will ever separate us."

By the end of my vows, we are crying again, but this time, I'm held against his strong chest. Glad I went with the waterproof eyeliner and mascara, I bury my face into his chest, and he buries his into my hair, inhaling each other's scent to calm us down.

"Sorry to interrupt Alpha, Luna, but we really should get the ceremony over with sometime today before the rain hits." The preacher whispers, bowing his head respectfully and causing us to laugh. The ceremony continues, and we say our I Do's to each other and finally hear our names pronounced. Tate wastes no time in pulling me close to kiss me passionately. The crowd starts cheering, hooting and yelling out things like "Take it to the bedroom" and "You go, Alpha" before we pull away, and he kisses my forehead.

The party is held inside the pack house. We walk into the ballroom as husband and wife, smiling when Tate pulled me close to dance to *I Was Made for Loving You* by Tori Kelly and Ed Sheeran, enjoying the moment between just us. We rarely leave each other side this night, and the pack members as well as our guests from allying packs are drunk and fast asleep by the time midnight hits. Chris and Jack took Julia to their house a while ago, wanting to let Tate and I have the night as a married couple to us. Slipping away from the drunken guests, Tate and I head home. We discard our formalwear piece by piece as we make our way to the bedroom. Finally, in bed, I find myself pinned under my husband, his thick cock buried deep inside me as he claims my body as his wife. The sounds of our pants and moans fill the house, continuing into the early morning as rays of light shine through the windows. I find myself held in his embrace, my energy fully spent, with Tate drawing lazy circles on my back.

"I noticed you never had anything to drink other than water, juice, and pop, care to tell me why?" Tate asks lazily, curiosity in his voice as he plays with my hair.

"What would you say to having another pup in the house?" I ask gently, drawing small circles on his chest and feeling him stiffen slightly.

"Do you mean...?" Tate asks with hopeful eyes his voice filled with disbelief.

"That Julia will be a big sister, yes." I finish his sentence with a chuckle. I squeak in surprise as I feel Tate roll us over, kissing me happily before moving to pepper kisses on my stomach.

"This is the best wedding gift ever, baby. I love you Laina Randall-Silvermoon." He whispers, tears glistening in his eyes. I smile and grab his face, pulling him towards me and kissing him lovingly.

"And I love you Tate Randall-Silvermoon." I whisper back, with my own tears rolling down my face and into my hair as I stare up at the man I love. My life is finally my own with the man in front of me as my partner forever. I was no longer the runaway Breeder. Now I am a mother, a wife, and a leader, and I have the perfect mate who has helped me more than I ever thought possible. I am Laina Randall-Silvermoon the Luna of Bloodsvain and not the runaway Breeder that changed my life forever.

THE END

ACKNOWLEDGEMENT

I would like to thank my friends and family for putting up with my nonstop rant of my book while I hid in my room or take over the dining room table to put my heart, soul and focus into revising the werewolf world of Laina Starcrest. An especial thanks to my mother who nurtured the book lover in me and battled with me to read at least one book a month as a child until she had to battle with me to go to bed late at night while I clutch some form of novel in my hands.

To my Wattpad followers who gave me input on cover designs and supporting me in the background anonymously behind their usernames cheering me on every step of the way from the first draft of "The Runaway Breeder" written in 2016 to where we are now in 2020 with double the word count and new depth behind a tale I have come to love.

Finally a huge thank you to my friend Sixpence Eastwood who not only kept me in line when editing and revising this novel but also took the time to read and edit "The Runaway Breeder". Without her making sure my easily distracted mind stays focused I would have never completed this novel in time to be published.

ABOUT THE AUTHOR

Alana Dyer

Born and raised in Brampton Ontario also known at "The Flower City" Alana Dyer started her relationship with books on a "Hate/Hate" relationship that quickly became a passion for reading as she found that novels can bring you places never seen before. It wasn't until 2015 with the discovery of Wattpad that Alana started writing seriously with the hopes of publishing. Now 5 years later she debuts on Amazon with her first full length novel "The Runaway Breeder" as well as a recipe book "Simply Desserts" with plans for many more to come.

BOOKS BY THIS AUTHOR

Rejection On The Full Moon

Soulless - werewolves who have turned rogue with no humanity left, giving in to their beastly urges.

Rejection - an act in which your soulmate rejects the mate bond, causing immense pain to the rejected.

These are the challenges Amberle Crest must overcome after becoming an outcast amongst the wolves her age due to an event outside of her control.

When her mate rejects her on her eighteenth birthday, Amberle realizes that living in a pack where the majority would rather use her as a slave than treat her as an equal is not worth the pain. She becomes the notorious wolf, Fire Foot, vowing that everyone would regret how they treated her, as she leaves her pack in the past.

Now a ghost forgotten by those that tormented her, Amberle does whatever it takes to survive as a lone wolf. A fateful day changes her lonely life to one full of happiness and hope--until ghosts from her own past call for aid in ridding their pack of the Soulless who threatens all wolf kind.

Faced with new friends, old foes, and the threat of a building army, will Amberle be able to fight the ghosts of her past to cherish the pack she has found or will an old mate claim her before a second chance mate can show her what being treasured by someone is all about?

Simple Desserts: Easy Dessert Recipes

We all love a sweet treat to enjoy, especially if its baked goods like a decadent cheese cake or a gooey chocolate chip cookie and with "Simply Desserts: Easy Dessert Recipes" you will soon be well on you way to baking sweet treats in no time with these 10 simple desserts that leaves room for you to be creative in the kitchen.Perfect for backyard parties or leaving a certain some one cookies at night during the holidays there is sure to be a recipe that will leave you wanting more.

The Best treat inside is the opportunity for you [the up-in-coming chef] to customize this book and write up to 10 of your own recipes or take pictures of your family and you creating lasting memories with each recipe you bake and place them inside the book.

CONTACT THE AUTHOR

CONTACT

alana.dyer.author@hotmail.com

http://amazon.com/author/alanadyer

Wattpad @Angel-Lunair

Alana Dyer

Author Alana Dyer

author.alana.dyer

Books available on Amazon Kindle
[E-book|Paperback]

A NEW SERIES

Take a look into her first book of a new series "The Rejection Series" and dive deeper into a world of werewolves, betrayal, finding ones true self and learning the meaning of true love.

Rejection Series Book 1: Rejection on the Full Moon

1. Once Upon A Time…NOT!

Do you know the stories of werewolves? Being that shift into wolf form on full moons with no choice in the matter? Where their animal instincts take over with bloodshed inevitable?

Those are true…well, everything but the full moon bullshit

My name is Amberle Crest, I am supposed to be a Beta or a Head Tracker due to my bloodline but you would never know.

I come from a modest pack, Forest Paw. Stupid name I know, but it is situated in the middle of the forest in north western Ontario close to a place humans love called Sauble Beach.

The thing about my pack was that it was a family, people loved you no matter who you are or what happened. Everyone is family and we help each other in times of need, or so they say.

I have never had any sort of family relationship past age eleven. The only familial love I gained in my life came from the Alpha, Blue. He treated me like family when he did not have any meetings or pack business that involved him to travel. When he was out of the territory my life was hell living. Since I was eleven

I knew a lot about how a pack could turn on you, even at a tender age. It was a horrible experience.

I was eighteen when my life finally took a turn for the better after crashing around me in a painful twist of fate.

But before I get ahead of myself, how about I start from the beginning?

2. The First Shift

SNAP

I whimper as my bones break and realign themselves.

"She's only six! She shouldn't be shifting till she is sixteen!" It was my mother, her voice laced with fear and worried. I knew that the fever I had been experiencing since last night was now not a cold or flu. My body decided that now would be the time I would shift into my wolf form for the first time.

SNAP

I cry out, my voice mixing with a howl. How could anyone expect a six-year-old to handle so much pain in one go. I know the risks of an early shift. Father made sure that the shift was a painful process and reassured my siblings and I that I would be fine when it happens at sixteen. But what I want at this moment is the pack doctor to come and numb me. Tears are forming in my eyes as I helplessly look towards my mother and father, begging for help.

"It just means our little Amber will be mated to an Alpha one day, maybe even a Royal." My father said with pride as he reassured my mom that everything would be alright. He hugs her briefly before bending down and holding a bottle of water with a straw to my lips.

"Drink Amberle, it'll help." I do as he tells me to and quickly drink as much of the cold liquid as fast as possible. He was right, it did help. But my skin felt like it was on fire, like it did when I accidentally scalded my foot with hot tea but ten times worse.

SNAP

My body contorted with pain as I shifted to all fours, my

body changing from human to wolf, the pain more unbearable than before. Tears were streaming down my face as my jaw becomes longer till it is a snout, teeth sharpen unnaturally and fur covers my skin.

SNAP

My mother leaves the room crying knowing that the possibility of me making it through the shift at this age is low.

GROWL

My father wipes away the sweat and blood from my forehead, causing the ears that shifted to the top of my head to flatten with pain.

SNAP

WHIMPER

SNAP

After what feels like an eternity of pain I slowly open my eyes to a new sensation. The house is quiet but I could sense my parents in the room. Their presence calling to me like a G.P.S signal. Something instinct told me to listen too.

"Honey, are you okay?" My mother's worried voice carries from across the room from where I was hiding. I whimpered slightly wanting to answer but finding I couldn't. It took me a moment until my mind wrapped around the fact that I was in wolf form. My tail thumps gently and I let out a soft whine. It was clear my parents were giving me space to learn about my second body, letting me test my limbs and focus on the new sensation of being lower to the ground. With courage I stand on wobbly legs, taking my first step before crashing to the floor and out of the safety of my hiding spot behind the kitchen island.

My parents gasp and I stared at their faces, their eyes wide with awe as they watched my movements as I struggle to stand again, my mother quickly helping me up and letting me use her body as support to stand.

"Amberle, you're beautiful. Maxwell, grab the full mirror from the hall way for our daughter to see herself." My mother exclaims happily, her hands in my fur and softly petting me. I give her a puzzled look as my father walks away to do what he is told.

After a few minutes he returns with the glass portion hidden from my view. Curiously I follow his movements until my eyes are blocked by my mother as the sounds of the mirror being set up reaches my ears. Finally things quiet down as I feel my small body being lead to a spot. I want to see what I look like.

"Tah-dah!" My mother moves out of the way and I face my reflection with shock and curiosity as a fluff ball of fur stares back at me in the reflection. From what I can see I was the size of a full grown medium dog, smaller than most werewolves who shift for the first time because I am only six but still bigger than I expected. In all honesty I should not have shifted at all for another ten years when a werewolf is mature and strong enough to handle the pain the first shift brings. The wolf in the mirror had fur like fire and it is this fur that mesmerizes me the most. Like the surface of the sun with multiple oranges, red and yellows it holds my attention in the reflection of the mirror and when I moved it swayed as if I am a ball of living fire...

Printed in Great Britain
by Amazon

66689997R00137